CHRISTMAS IN MELTDOWN

When her assistant suddenly quits, struggling bistro owner Lucy is filled with despair. Top chef James rides to the rescue — but Lucy fears he's hijacking her menus. As electricity fizzes between the two, and festive delights fly from the kitchen, Lucy faces a business dilemma. Does James hold the key to success? Snow poses fresh challenges as each cook falls more deeply in love with the other. Will it be James or Lucy who melts first?

Books by Jill Barry
in the Linford Romance Library:

DREAMS OF YESTERDAY
GIRL WITH A GOLD WING
THE SECRET OF THE
SILVER LOCKET
A CHRISTMAS ENGAGEMENT
MRS ROBINSON
CHRISTMAS REVELATIONS

JILL BARRY

CHRISTMAS IN MELTDOWN

Complete and Unabridged

LINFORD
Leicester

First published in Great Britain in 2015

First Linford Edition
published 2016

*A catalogue record for this book is available
from the British Library.*

ISBN 978–1–4448–3052–1

Published by
F. A. Thorpe (Publishing)
Anstey, Leicestershire

Set by Words & Graphics Ltd.
Anstey, Leicestershire
Printed and bound in Great Britain by
T. J. International Ltd., Padstow, Cornwall

This book is printed on acid-free paper

1

Mistletoe and Mulled Wine? Or breath-taking Christmas Cocktails? Lucy Stephenson, clattering downstairs to work, was trying to decide on appropriately festive themes when her ring tone trilled.

'Hi, Alfonso.' Lucy couldn't help smiling at the Italian's cheerful tones. She hovered, straining to hear his voice over the indoor market's hubbub. 'Brilliant. I spent yesterday turning the bistro into a winter wonderland, so I'll head over when Emily arrives,' she said. 'And no, you can't have a double espresso.'

Lucy continued walking, shaking her head at Alfonso's banter. 'Stop flirting! I'll see you soon. Ciao!'

Lucy could just picture Alfonso's wife at the other end, also shaking her head in despair. She had become fond of the couple over the years; she even used to babysit their beautiful twin daughters on rare free nights. Alfonso's offer to reserve some of his best wares was helpful, especially now, struggling to keep her bistro popular. Lucy was keeping everything crossed that the takings for December would bring tidings of comfort and joy to her bank manager.

She opened the connecting door to the business. Living in the heart of Dexford suited her, as did arriving at work without stepping outside. In her office, she fired up her laptop, blowing on her fingers before tapping at the keyboard.

Hearing the outer door open and shut, she called out, 'Morning, Em. I'll do the market run if you want to grab a cuppa. Afterwards, we need to talk.'

Lucy paused. Emily was taking her time.

'What are you doing? Admiring my festive décor? Not too much tinsel, I hope!'

It wasn't like Emily to ignore a greeting. Usually, she responded with a 'Hello, boss' before complaining about her bus journey or the awful takeout tea she'd squandered hard-earned cash on.

Lucy's heart skipped a beat. Maybe it wasn't Emily? It was unlikely, as Em was the only other key-holder, but how terrible if an invader crashed into the office, shouting, 'Freeze!'

But no — Lucy's sous chef and sounding board, the employee who'd become a friend, appeared in the doorway. She wore her usual turquoise fleece with a black wool scarf swathing her shoulders. But she didn't smile. Nor did she seem able to find her tongue.

And how about that expression on her face? The one making her look as if she'd won the Lottery, but must swim across a shark-infested lake to claim her prize. Lucy jumped up and pulled out a chair.

'Whatever it is, we can sort it, Em.' *Whatever it is, it can't be worse than the bistro's fragile financial state.* 'Sit down and tell me what's wrong.' Lucy perched on the edge of the head teacher's desk that, spotted in an antiques shop, she'd just had to buy.

Emily sat. 'Lucy,' she said, 'I know this won't be easy for you to hear, but it's only right I say it to your face.' She laced her fingers together on her lap.

She's trying to stop trembling. 'Go on, Em.'

The girl took a deep breath. 'I'm leaving.'

'What?'

'I'm going away.'

'Yes, I heard — I just don't quite understand.'

'I'm leaving Dexford for good, Lucy. I'm sorry, but it's what I want.'

'Wow.' Lucy swallowed hard. 'When? How much notice are you giving me? One month? Two?'

'I have to go today.'

Lucy tried to breathe slowly, despite the tidal wave roaring in her ears. 'But . . . you can't! I've misunderstood, haven't I? Please tell me I'm hearing things.'

Emily shook her head. 'We fly out to Majorca this afternoon.'

Lucy stopped perching and crossed to the window, where she stood, staring at the narrow side street without seeing it. 'So this is about Nic.' It was a statement, not a question. She turned to face her friend.

'I need to go with him, Lucy.'

'I still don't understand. You were due to visit his family in the New Year anyway, why on earth couldn't you have waited just a few more weeks for your fix of winter sunshine? And what — suddenly it's a permanent move? What are you both thinking? Never mind his job and yours. Never mind loyalty to your colleagues.' Lucy felt as if she'd been slapped in the face.

'It's not like that. You know I wouldn't leave you in the lurch unless I really had to.'

'I honestly don't know what to think. I don't understand. Is this all about the

'L' word, or is it a career change for him and you're just going along for the ride?'

'It'll be a career change for both of us, and it's not about winter sunshine. His father's been admitted to hospital. Nic was on Skype with his brother for most of yesterday. Like you said, we'd already booked to go to Palma after Christmas; Nic's just changed our flight.'

Emily stopped talking to her hands and raised her head to meet Lucy's gaze. 'It's a crisis, but it's helped us focus on our future. Please try and be happy for me. Nic's asked me to marry him, and we'll run the family restaurant together while we see what happens with his father.'

'Congratulations. I'm over the moon for you,' said Lucy bitterly, feeling awful about Nic's father, but unable to get past the feeling that Emily could have handled the situation better.

She moved behind her desk and sat opposite Emily. 'I'm sorry about Nic's father, of course I am. Obviously, I'll credit your bank account with salary owing,' she said, looking down at her desk. 'You realise, of course, what an enormous strain you're placing upon your colleagues.' She paused to let this sink in, then added, 'And upon me. I thought we were friends.'

Emily opened her mouth, but clearly couldn't find anything to say.

Lucy exhaled a shaky breath, then held out her hand, palm upwards. 'I'll have my key back, please. The moment you've cleared your locker, I'd appreciate your getting out of my sight.'

* * *

Lucy pulled down her red woollen hat to eyebrow level and let herself out into the bone-chilling morning. She'd allowed herself some private tears but couldn't afford self-pity, even if Emily's announcement had rocked her world.

Students lounged at the bus stop, chatting and checking phones, probably moaning about course deadlines. If only she could magic away fifteen years and jump on the bus with them.

A coach-load of school children, their faces pale blobs behind tinted windows, waited in a traffic queue. Perhaps the students were off to a stately home to experience a Tudor Christmas. Whatever they were doing, she was sure it would be much more fun than the day she faced.

Men and women hurried along the pavements. For most, today was an ordinary, dank December Tuesday. For Lucy, it was like stepping blindfold into the future.

She dived through the market's archway, trying to stop obsessing about Emily and instead focus on solving this setback. She paused for a moment, closing her eyes and letting the familiar noises and aromas encircle her. Traders had sold their wares within this building since Victorian times.

Holding her head high, she headed for her favourite greengrocer.

'Hey, Lucy.' The stallholder, muffled in multi-coloured layers, peered round a towering heap of holly. 'Don't look so worried! It might never happen.'

'Maybe it already has, Maggie.'

'You want to talk about it, honey?'

'Not right now, thanks. It's just something I need to think through. A bit of a staffing disaster.'

'Well, you know where to come for help. I have a niece home from Uni, she's helping out while my regular lady's off sick. If you need someone to run errands and load the dishwasher, just say the word.'

'Brilliant, Maggie. I'll bear it in mind.' Lucy selected fresh herbs and a string of garlic. Once she got back to The Town Mouse, she needed to call the agency.

She dodged down the side of the hall, avoiding the crowds, to reach Alfonso and Celeste's fish stall. Here she felt like sobbing out her troubles to the warmhearted couple. But what good would that do? They too were busy and, despite her gloom, she pasted a smile on her face and hoped she sounded cheerful.

The Town Mouse had already catered for its first rush of annual office parties, and more were booked for the following Friday and Saturday. This was such an important time of year and she couldn't afford to let standards slip. Even regular patrons could easily go elsewhere, if she couldn't provide the wow factor. Ruefully, she thought of the names missing from her forward bookings this year.

She hurried across the road, dodging between vehicles waiting for the lights to change. She might feel better when she spoke to her favourite administrator at the agency. Dustin had visited her restaurant and knew her rigorous requirements. But deep inside, where demons lurked, Lucy harboured a dark thought. With the days counting down until the big 'C,' what chef worth his or her salt would be available to start work immediately?

2

With her free hand, Lucy brought up the luncheon reservations page on her laptop.

'I could really do without it, Dustin. This time of year brings enough problems, without a major player missing.'

'I so know where you're coming from,' came the heartfelt reply. 'A 'flu outbreak is my worst nightmare. And sometimes bar staff and waiters find the hype and hurly-burly too much and they up and run. Tell me, is the lovely Marco still with you?'

'Yes, thank goodness. He shows a lot of promise, but I can't expect him to carry too much responsibility.'

'Give the guy a chance to step up, maybe? He might surprise you. Meanwhile I'll see what I can do. Shall I find you another commis chef while Marco finds his feet?'

'Okay, let's do that,' said Emily. 'But on the understanding it's a temporary position.'

'I do have another suggestion, though you'll probably slam the phone down.'

'Come on, Dustin. These are desperate times.'

'I have a head chef who describes himself as a trouble shooter.'

Lucy sighed. 'Don't tell me Gordon Ramsay's job hunting!'

'At least you still have your sense of humour.'

'Only just. But do you mean a trouble shooter like they have on those TV reality shows?' She didn't wait for an answer. 'Because what I need is someone who can cook with a capital C. Someone experienced enough to help save my business and my sanity — don't dare tell anyone I said that . . . '

'As if!' Dustin interjected.

'And I can do without a bad-boy chef insisting on a salary to match his king-size ego.'

'Who said anything about him being a bad boy? This guy has the kind of experience you're after, in spades. Plus, he's free just now and looking round for a good kitchen.'

'No troubles left for him to shoot?'

'He had to take a couple of months out. Personal reasons.'

Lucy's heart sank. Emotional baggage wasn't a helpful addition to a chef's CV.

'If he's that wonderful, he'll be wanting top dollar, surely?'

'He told me if he liked the restaurant, he'd be willing to compromise, in the short term.'

'Is that right? What's his name?'

'James Drummond. Look, I have to go out soon. If you decide to interview, call back and say I recommended him.'

'Okay. But I doubt I'll make that speedy a decision.'

'I'll email you his CV. Just have a think about it.'

'Well, I suppose it'll do no harm to check him out.'

She closed the call. Her remaining employees were arriving and she needed to break the news and give them a pep talk. She had no concerns about anyone's ability, but everyone needed to crank it up a gear while Lucy ensured the festive razzmatazz didn't flop like an undercooked soufflé.

* * *

'Blimey, who'd have thought it?'

'My sentiments exactly, Vicki.'

Lucy and her team sat at the big table used for groups or for solo customers feeling sociable. Her gaze roamed over them all, then returned to the person who was about to receive a second shock.

'Marco, I need you to cover the sous chef role temporarily, while I sort things out.'

Marco gasped.

'Thank you, Chef. I'll try not to let you down.'

'I know that. I'm hoping to find

someone to replace Emily, but it'll be good to have you beside me, at least during this settling-in period.'

Lucy turned to Shaz.

'How do you feel about stepping up? The agency's sending someone with a similar CV to Marco, but if you could take responsibility for most of the desserts, it'd be a tremendous help.'

'Wow.' Shaz's cheeks turned pink. 'I'll do my best.'

'Thank you. And everyone, please remember this: I'm proud of my team, and I expect nothing less than the best performance from each and every one of you. Because that's always been the case, hasn't it?' She looked at them, expectantly.

'For sure,' said Leanne, the bistro's bar manager.

'Absolutely,' said Vicki.

'One hundred per cent agree,' said Marco.

'We value our jobs,' said Tilly solemnly. 'Don't we, Josh?'

'You bet.'

Lucy smiled at her team. 'Thank you.'

'I'd like to get started now, if that's okay?' Marco rose, taking his coffee mug with him.

Lucy swallowed hard. She had a lot to be thankful for. But they'd all need a lot more than enthusiasm to survive this, the most frenetic fortnight of the year.

* * *

James Drummond wrapped himself in a thick towelling gown and pushed his feet into suede slippers. December seemed hell bent on churning out colder than usual weather, but he'd found New York even more bone-chillingly icy.

James never again wanted to experience anything like those weeks he'd gone through since receiving news of Sam's accident. His son's mum, Cassie, had coped brilliantly, even finding time to comfort the lovely family of Sam's school friend, with whom Sam had been spending the day when the accident happened. And now, broken bones were healing and the little boy's spirit remained intact, though he was left with a metal pin inside one arm.

'I'm bionic, Daddy!' The words echoed in James' head and, not for the first time, he contemplated sub-letting his London flat to seek a job and somewhere to live in New York, even if just for a few years, so he could play a significant part in Sam's upbringing. Something told him, though, that Cassie might not take this in the way it was intended. Accidents happened, and in no way could Cassie have prevented this one — but James suspected his former wife might interpret such a move on his part as some kind of judgement on her mothering skills.

He checked his emails. One from Dustin, a guy at the catering agency James had registered with on returning from the States. When that awful call had come from Cassie, he'd had to pull out of the contract he'd been due to start; now, back home, he was temporarily adrift.

Hey, James! Superb opportunity with big hotel chain London area — made for you! Or, how about a bistro in Dexford? Sous chef left without notice. Owner's a tad prickly. Great food. Office parties. Huge potential. Lucy NEEDS someone like YOU. Four weeks minimum while we seek permanent chef.

James rubbed his stubbly chin. The bistro gig sounded interesting, but how about that sub-text? If Dustin considered James the kind of chef this place needed, maybe the engine was idling. He'd seen it happen many times. It was easy to take one's clientele for granted.

Even so, he felt this might be a challenge to relish. Plus, the owner must be frantic. With Christmas round the corner, Dustin might be able to negotiate a half-decent pay rate. He could do with a cash injection, especially as, towards the end of his stay, Cassie had allowed him to treat the three of them to a fortnight at a Florida hotel with more stars than the Milky Way. They'd taken a suite and Sam was thrilled at having both his mom and dad around. To James' relief, Cassie's boyfriend had shown enough sensitivity to stay out of the equation. As lovely as it had been to see his son so happy, that, plus a couple of months with no job, had taken its toll on his bank balance.

Not for the first time since Cassie had shattered his world by deciding to return to her homeland and raise their son in New York, James wondered how much she'd ever really loved him. Or even how much he'd really loved her. But his practical side warned it was too late for psychobabble.

He responded to Dustin's message. *OK. Interested in bistro. Name?*

By the time he'd had juice, a bagel and coffee from his machine, Dustin's reply arrived, prompting James to type The Town Mouse into his search engine. Several options came up in the London area, plus one in Dexford. James gazed at the screen, waiting for the bistro website to talk to him. It didn't. Yet Dustin had described the food as great. He clicked on the menu section.

'Interesting,' he said aloud. They ran a Throwback Thursday menu, this week offering Toad in the Hole, onion gravy with carrots and roast potatoes. The non-meat option was spinach, chestnut and blue cheese en croute.

'But what a load of boring puddings.' James flipped to the Christmas menu. It offered a choice of three starters and main courses. James noted the English plum pudding, but silently struck Black Forest Gateau and Sherry Trifle from the list. There was a limit to what Retro did for an eating establishment.

He glanced at Menu of the Day and groaned. No offence to senior citizens, but who was the bistro targeting? Trying to please everyone didn't usually come off. He wondered why the owner had been let down in such spectacular fashion. He'd never, ever pull a stunt like that. No wonder Dustin had described her as prickly — it was hardly surprising, considering. She must be in shock, and who could blame her? On the other hand, maybe this Lucy was the sort who devoured her sous chefs for breakfast. And would she seriously contemplate employing a head chef after years working with a sous? Although, if The Town Mouse was as outstanding as Dustin puffed it up to be, she'd have to do something — how the heck would one chef, however experienced, handle lunches plus evening dinner service?

James Drummond's antennae weren't just twitching, they were in overdrive. He noted the bistro's address and researched train times. He couldn't explain why this situation so intrigued him, but he'd learn a lot from a visit; and if he disliked what he saw, he wouldn't fritter his or the owner's time by requesting an interview.

* * *

So far, Lucy felt all was going well. Cue hollow laugh. Lunch service hadn't even begun. She'd whizzed through fish preparation, slicing fillets into bite-sized pieces. Made a glossy roux. Awarded a virtual gold star to Marco for creating a fluffy cloud of mashed potatoes and a heap of chopped herbs. The young man usually kept his cool, but in the two years he'd worked for her, Lucy hadn't ever before thrown him so completely in at the deep end. She kept the thought to herself. Like Dustin said, Marco might yet surprise her.

Her bar manager appeared, set to collect lemons, limes and bagged-up ice cubes. Leanne, serene and experienced, not only orchestrated the drinks service but also dealt with stock ordering.

'All well, Lucy?'

'Ask me again round about two-thirty.'

Leanne closed the freezer door. 'You'll be fine. We're not usually that busy on Tuesdays, are we?'

'Just as well, because I've no idea how long it'll take to replace Emily.'

'You'll find a temp, surely? There's always someone out there.'

'Yes, but this is peak time. I'm wary as to why a chef with excellent qualifications would be available.'

Leanne hoisted her tray. 'Stuff happens.'

'That's what worries me.'

Leanne raised an eyebrow. 'You need to think positive, Lucy. Someone might've been working somewhere that suddenly folded.'

'Probably because of its miserable menu.'

'Sometimes, through no fault of our own, personal situations throw us off course.'

True. Think of Emily.

'There could be a chef out there who'd be perfect for The Town Mouse,' Leanne continued. 'He or she might've quit a job to sort out family problems. What does Dustin say?'

'He has a prospect. A head chef willing to do sous if he feels it's right for him.'

'Unusual. When do you interview?'

'Let's get today over and done with, first. You're right, Leanne, and thank you — I think I'm still just reeling from shock.'

* * *

James Drummond left Dexford's train station and wandered along the high street. Having spotted the market building, he decided to investigate before visiting The Town Mouse.

He caught the eye of a young woman surrounded by shiny baubles and flashy, glittery decorations that he knew Sam would adore.

'Hey, could I ask which stall you buy your fish from?' he said, smiling at her.

'Aw, and there was I hoping to tempt you with a bumper bag of tinsel.' She winked at him.

'I'm a minimalist.'

'Pity. Well, I use Martin's, just beyond the tea bar.' She waved at the nearby cafe. 'But if you want more than a pair of kippers or a cone of shrimps, you should try Severini's, down the end. They're the bee's knees.'

'Thanks,' he said. 'And I'm sorry to let you down on the tinsel; I've no use for decorations.'

'Not a family man, then?'

He hesitated. She was extremely pretty and wore no rings except a fine silver nose hoop.

'It's a long story.'

'Isn't it always?' She turned to take a customer's money. 'Well, the name's Jasmine. You know where I am if you feel a sudden need to deck the halls in your mansion — or maisonette.'

James walked on. Gorgeous Jasmine had fluttered her eyelashes. He reminded himself he was seeking a job, not some-one to date. All that malarkey seemed far too much hassle.

He found a couple of greengrocery stalls, both looking okay. He checked out a display of jellied eels and other delicacies, before noticing the name Severini emblazoned on the back wall. He lost no time in examining the remaining produce and liked what he saw.

When the female half of the couple serving turned to him with a welcoming smile, James held up his hand.

'I'm sorry, I'm not buying. This is cheeky, but would you mind telling me which local restaurants you supply? I'm in the trade and I can see how important top quality produce is to you.'

The woman's eyes sparkled. 'Thank you, sir. We supply more than one business around here, but our best customer is The Town Mouse. That's the bistro further up the high street.'

'I'm about to sample their lunch menu, if they can fit me in.'

'You should be fine if you go now, except it's the time of year for office parties. How about you say Celeste recommended you?'

'Cheers. If I'm back in the area, I'll make a point of buying my dinner from you.'

'You don't have your own business?'

He shook his head. 'I'm a freelance chef. I like short-term contracts. Get in. Revolutionise. Get out.'

She looked him up and down. 'I don't think The Town Mouse needs revolutions. Lucy and Emily work their socks off and they have a superb team. The food is *bellissima*.'

'That's good to hear. See you, Celeste.'

James headed for the exit. So, the bistro owner was keeping shtum over her current predicament? Understandable. No chef wanted to cast a shadow over their culinary reputation. He'd known better than to reveal his awareness of the true circumstances. Next, he needed to get his feet under a table and sample the cuisine.

* * *

'So far so good?'

'These fish pies are turning a lovely golden brown.'

Lucy looked at the clock. 'Maybe you should take five. And, Shaz, while I speak to Leanne, can you stir the soup please? Maybe lower the heat?'

'Okay, Chef.' Shaz put down her spoon. 'This spiced fruit compote smells heavenly.'

'It's a perfect lunchtime pudding. Put up ten would you, after you've sorted the soup? They can go in the big fridge. The topping's already chilling?'

'Yes, Chef.'

'Lovely.' She pushed through the swing doors in search of her bar manager. Leanne looked immaculate in a black dress and scarlet cummerbund, long blonde hair scooped into a chignon.

'I think we're good to go.' Lucy glanced at the door. 'You can turn the sign round. The first bookings are for noon, aren't they?'

'They are.'

'I'll make myself scarce.'

Lucy hurried past tables laid for lunch. At the centre of each stood a small ceramic pot holding sprigs of holly, their dark green leaves and vivid red berries contrasting beautifully with the pristine white table cloths. The background music was as upmarket a Christmas medley as Lucy could locate.

On her way, she heard the street door open. This was the point — bridging the chasm between empty tables and buzzing bistro — at which her mouth usually dried. Funny how it wasn't the case just then. Perhaps she was beyond nervousness.

'Where's Shaz?' Lucy asked Marco as she saw him leaving the rest room. 'Taking five?'

He reddened. 'I think she might've, um, fainted, Chef.'

Lucy stood, hands on hips, knowing her mouth made a perfect 'O' as she realised her designated first-aider was en route to Gatwick Airport.

'She's lying on the couch; that's why

I was coming to get you.'

'Call Vicki, please. And take those pies out before golden turns to charcoal!'

Lucy pushed open the rest room door and knelt beside her employee.

'Hey, sweetie?' She felt Shaz's fore-head. She looked pale but she wasn't feverish. Phew.

Shaz opened her eyes. 'I fainted, didn't I?'

'You did. Have you been fasting again?'

'No way.'

'Maybe too much to drink last night? Though that's not like you.'

'It's not alcohol that's my problem. I think I'm fine, now, Chef.'

Shaz struggled to sit up as Vicki arrived. She put her hands to her head.

'Ooh, bad mistake.'

'Leave her to me, Lucy,' said Vicki. 'I think I know what the problem is, and it's nothing catching.'

'That's a relief. Shaz, if you can't work, Vicki will call a cab.'

'No! I'll be fine in a few minutes. Please don't worry about me, either of you. I won't move until I feel ready, but I won't desert you if I can help it.'

Lucy had a fair idea what ailed Shaz, but this was no time to talk dates or counsel her employee. She hurried back to her workspace. So much for her previous calculations. She, Marco, and young Josh, who was still on probation, were now left to tackle the flood of food orders about to deluge them.

3

James pushed open the elegant, sea-green door, wondering why he felt a sensation similar to the first time he'd gone on a blind date.

He stood at the ubiquitous sign requesting patrons to wait, his gaze taking in the foyer carpeting, also sea green, and the barely pink walls. Classy. And tons better in real life than in the picture on the website. So that needed sorting.

He didn't have to wait long before a tall girl, with hair cut in a neat black bob, glided forward and smiled, cherry-glossed lips revealing enviably white teeth. Her name badge introduced her as Tilly.

'Do you have a table reservation, sir?'

James shook his head. 'Sadly, not. I'm on my own, so if you have a spare corner, Tilly, it would be great.'

He was aware of the effect his chocolate-brown eyes could have on women. Hadn't his ex-wife mentioned this more than once? Of course, Cassie hadn't meant it as a compliment.

'I'll need to check, but I'm sure we can do better than that for you.'

'If it helps, a lady called Celeste suggested I mention her name.'

Tilly's lips twitched. 'Just one tiny moment.' She hastened to the bar and consulted the elegant woman putting a bottle of wine on ice. James recognised it as being from the list of one of his favourite French houses — not as famous as some, but known for superb quality.

The bar manager glanced across and nodded to Tilly who returned at once. It would seem they were fussy about their chance clientele. James wore black denim jeans, a grey sweater and black leather jacket, not having felt inclined to turn up looking like a City boy.

'There's a table for two available but

it's a bit tucked away. Or you're welcome to sit at the communal table in the middle.'

'Is 'tucked away' shorthand for 'on the flight path to the toilets'?'

Tilly's eyes widened. 'Definitely not. It's in a corner, sir. We usually reserve it for couples who we think really should go get a room.'

James laughed. 'Well, as you have no solo tables and I'd hate to deprive someone of a romantic luncheon rendezvous, maybe I'll go for the communal option.' He might observe while he ate or he might become engaged in conversation. New customers or regulars, it didn't matter, their opinions would be a good barometer.

Seated, he requested a large glass of house red and turned his attention to the menu. When the phone on the bar rang, he thought nothing of it, interested only in how nicely the bistro filled up.

They did a good lunchtime trade. And then some. They'd be shoehorning customers in soon and, unless the proprietor had found someone to fill the shoes of her assistant, he had the uneasy feeling the wheels might start to fall off the wagon. If his premonition proved correct, the chef would be under incredible pressure, striving to keep orders rolling smooth as honey off a spoon.

He couldn't help notice the apprehensive look on the bar manager's face when she passed his table and whooshed through the service doors. She returned barely a minute later, having had, he knew, a confab with the boss. The woman resumed her place and began filling a drinks order, hands moving deftly, expression tranquil. A pro.

James wasn't prepared for the street door to open, allowing about twenty people to stream through and cluster in the foyer while Tilly did her best to accommodate them. Some held reservations. Some didn't. Several people, including an elderly couple, headed for the table where he sat. The husband pulled out a chair for his wife and seated himself opposite James.

'Well, this is jolly.' The newcomer, who wore a red corduroy jacket and red and white bow tie, eyed James. 'Are you one of the poor unfortunates staying at the hotel up the road too?'

'No,' said James. 'Is there a problem?'

'The central heating system is malfunctioning. The missus and I could have told them that. We woke up this morning to find penguins dancing round the bed.'

James gave the man's wife a sympathetic smile. 'Poor you. The temperature can't be far above freezing.'

'My wife wants to go shopping. We thought we'd save a pound or two and stay away from the rip-off hotels.'

James saw the wife roll her eyes.

'Okay, it was me who decided we'd stay in the outback,' said Mr Bow Tie. 'It's not a bad journey in, and our hotel's fine otherwise. They've assured us it'll be sorted soon; meantime, we thought we'd find somewhere for a bite to eat and a warm up.'

'Did someone recommend coming here?' James asked.

'Yes, but I wonder whether we'd have done better to go straight to Piccadilly Circus. Looks like this place is filling up.'

James read the innuendo. Tolerance level was already low. Probably the long-suffering wife was cheesed off and had given her old fella a hard time for not booking a hotel nearer the top department stores. They wanted a menu; they wanted a glass of red wine to cheer them up; and they were wary at the prospect of waiting for a meal that might be a long time coming, given the sudden customer rush.

James imagined The Town Mouse usually glided along like Santa's sledge on a moonlit Yuletide. But the words 'log jam' flashed into his consciousness, as surely as though he was driving along a motorway and suddenly seeing a stream of brake lights ahead.

He made a decision. He might get his head bitten off. He might find himself banned before even tasting a spoonful of soup. But his temperament wouldn't let him sit still, on the brink of a crisis, without offering his services.

'I'm sure someone will be with you soon.' Carefully he lifted his wineglass and placed it between Mr Bow Tie and his missus. 'Have that on me! I haven't touched it, and there's an urgent matter I must deal with.'

He was off before anyone could say a word, striding towards the kitchen and pushing open the swing doors. James stood, gazing at a familiar scene, even as he realised his action wasn't only hot-headed, but flouted health and safety regulations.

He saw the chef whip her head round as the doors swung shut, her beautiful blue eyes widening in shock. Something pinged in his brain. He had to get a word in before she pressed a panic button. Or kicked him out.

* * *

When Leanne told her about the call from the hotel up the road, Lucy had wanted to say a big NO. NO. NO! All those extra people heading their way wanting lunch! But what was she in business for, if not to feed people and make a profit? Her quandary was having her team reduced by two.

'Get Tilly to ask if some of them would like to wait in the foyer with a complimentary glass of wine,' she said. *Funny how my voice sounds so confident when my insides are churning.*

'If anyone fails to honour their reservation,' said Leanne, 'we can upgrade people already here. The chips are down, aren't they?'

'Absolutely,' said Lucy. 'Make it clear to Tilly: any problem, you're the one to deal with it.' She forced a smile. 'What's keeping you?'

Leanne hurried away.

'Marco?' Lucy called to her assistant. 'The good news is, we're expecting an overflow of disappointed hotel guests — don't ask.'

'And the bad news, Chef?'

'It's too late to get more help, so it's down to you, me and Josh. And breathe!'

She watched Marco stand straighter.

'Josh,' he called. 'If I ask you to do something, just do it. Chef yells at you to do something, just do it, and never mind what I just asked you to do. Got it?'

'Got it,' said Josh.

'Four soups,' said Lucy.

'Got it,' said Marco.

Lucy slipped into her usual routine, plating up fish pie and side vegetables. The waiting team were doing their job, so no worries there. It was the kitchen production line where the potential danger lurked, ready to coil sneaky tentacles round the key players and drag them under. She prayed that wouldn't happen.

Used crockery began cluttering the pristine stainless steel surfaces.

'Josh, get that out of the way, please.' Lucy knew if she didn't keep her customary cool, the only way was down. She ran a courteous kitchen; if she couldn't achieve politeness, how could she expect her staff to do so?

'Two more beef entrecote,' she muttered, pouring spicy, herby, garlicky sauce over medium-rare steaks.

'More chips.' Marco, moving as if on roller blades, arrived before she could sound the alert.

'You're a star,' she said. 'Who's looking after the soup?'

'Josh, please get that pan back over a low heat,' said Marco. 'Customers are still ordering their first course.'

Lucy glanced at the waiting orders. An icy dagger pierced her heart. Vicki entered the kitchen, calling that a customer had asked for a side order of chips with his fish pie. Lucy gritted her teeth. Some people had no notion of nutrition.

'What's that smell?' She heard herself shouting as though from a distance. 'Someone check those chips!'

'We need more bread.' Vicki stood, looking this way and that. 'What's happened to the system?'

'Should these apple pies go in now, Chef?'

Lucy was desperately behind. She needed to stay focused but she was on the ropes. How could they hope to handle this sudden rush when her team wasn't co-ordinating?

Maybe this wasn't really happening. Maybe she was in the midst of a nightmare. No such luck, because here was someone else pushing through the doors. She turned her head and bumped gazes with a stranger standing inside the split doors.

She sucked in her breath. If he'd invaded her domain to complain about poor service, she'd say this was an emergency and he should consider elderly patrons arriving, rubbing their hands and stamping their feet. Their need for sustenance far exceeded that of a man who looked nowhere near elderly. Or cold. This much, at least, Lucy registered.

The visitor held up his hands. 'Lucy? Please don't send me away. I'm a chef and it looks like you could use some help. Where can I scrub up and cover up?'

His calm, caramel tones could soothe a ravening horde. Maybe she needed to cut this usurper a little slack. Could he really be serious?

'If it's any help, Celeste sent me.'

How did Celeste know? Confused, Lucy opened her mouth to speak.

'Cool,' said Marco. 'Follow me, Chef.'

So Marco was giving the orders round here now? But Lucy didn't argue. She didn't have time. She continued plating up meals as if programmed. Trying to think for everyone else.

In a twinkling, the stranger returned, wearing, Lucy imagined, Marco's spare chef's uniform. She heard him ask Josh his name, then say: 'Well, Josh, unless you mop up that dollop of soup by your left foot, we're looking at an accident. Move, please!'

The man was alongside now. She caught a whiff of aftershave, something fresh and tangy, yet with a powerful note, whirling her deep inside a pine forest. Or a lemon grove. Yes. Surrounded by ripe lemons nestling among green leaves.

What was the matter with her? Who cared what brand of toiletries this guy favoured? She seemed to have lost the power of speech. Again.

He reached down the next order, moving smoothly, without requesting guidance. He might be a stranger to her but he was no stranger to this demanding, addictive, sometimes frustrating — make that often frustrating — creative art of food production.

Why on earth would Celeste have

sent him? Lucy was convinced she hadn't let slip one word about Emily's dramatic departure. It didn't make sense. But slowly the orders backlog diminished and Lucy began thinking she might survive this torture. Except it was no torture working beside this nameless man that, surely, Lucy's guardian angel must have propelled into her orbit.

Shaz obviously didn't feel well enough to work. Someone should check on her. Vicki appeared, and must have read Lucy's mind, because she darted into the rest room and returned at once, announcing, 'Shaz is asleep.'

'Your staff get to sleep on duty?' The stranger spoke out of the side of his mouth but those rich chocolate tones still managed to rattle Lucy's composure.

'It's a long story.' She wasn't about to explain her predicament. All she wanted was for him to stay with her. Between them, there existed the unspoken need to present an unruffled front. This chef had appeared from nowhere at the precise instant Lucy had feared she might lose the plot. For having saved her, she'd be eternally grateful — but they had plenty to do yet.

* * *

'This fish pie is not at all bad.'

'I'll take that as a compliment, shall I?'

'Hmm. I was beginning to worry you'd sell it all before I had a chance to sample it.'

She eyed him across the big table, where the two of them sat at either end. Her staff always ate early and she and the maverick chef were alone in the afternoon downtime. Lucy knew she should ask for ID, maybe even have asked Marco to hang around, but she needed him up and running that evening.

Luckily they had a block booking, which meant a menu chosen up front. A local women's organisation had matinee tickets for a jukebox musical in

London's West End, and they had opted to return to The Town Mouse so they could eat and drink and enjoy an easy trip home instead of tackling escalators and trains. The evening should be a doddle after that Titanic experience earlier.

'I don't even know your name.'

'Does that matter?'

'It seems rude, not calling you anything.'

He shrugged. Laid down his fork.

'Chef will do.'

'Well, you got me out of a huge predicament, Chef. I take it you'll accept cash in hand?'

He pursed his lips. 'I don't expect payment. In fact, I owe you for a large glass of house red I gave away.'

'Forget it. But why put yourself out for someone you don't know?'

'You're a talented cook and you've built a good reputation.'

Only good?

'I couldn't sit out here earlier, making small talk, knowing what you must be going through. Call it comradely concern.'

Lucy's insides flipped. *Concentrate!*

'I still don't understand why you turned up. Was it sheer chance? When I asked you before, you changed the subject.'

'Let's just say I had business in the area. I decided to call and ask for a table and I got lucky.'

Huh. With that voice and those gorgeous brown eyes, I'm not surprised — Tilly would've been a melting mass of jelly in your hands!

Lucy swallowed hard.

'I'd say I'm the one who got lucky. You wouldn't happen to want a job, would you?'

There, she'd said it. She'd unleashed the idea that had been simmering at the back of her mind ever since he crashed into her kitchen like a culinary Clint Eastwood, minus the poncho and cheroot — The Chef With No Name.

He didn't answer her question.

'Here's the thing,' she continued. 'I

don't usually have staff problems, but my sous chef arrived this morning and announced she was about to jet off abroad with her fiancé. Just like that. Then the world and his wife turned up.'

'I heard about the hotel.'

'Did you? As for Shaz, I'd just decided to upgrade her when she flaked out. I have a hunch she'll be putting in for maternity leave before long.' She drank some water.

'That is rough luck.'

'Getting pregnant?'

'Having your sous walk out on you without notice.'

'I think we'll survive tonight. Shaz swore she'd be fine for her evening shift and Marco's displaying nerves of steel. Fair play, Dustin did suggest that might happen.'

'Um, Dustin?'

'He's the agency guy I deal with. Speaking of which, I seem to remember asking whether you'd consider working for me?' She counted to ten. 'No, I thought I couldn't get that lucky. I suppose this must be your day off?'

He gestured to the cafetière. 'Top up?'

She shook her head. 'You go ahead. So, do I take it you're not interested in a temporary job?'

'I have a decision to make. I won't attend any interview unless I'm confident I fit the role and I like the establishment.'

Almost without realising, Lucy had made one of those little fortune-telling thingies from a paper napkin. It flopped about a bit, but it worked. Kind of. Of course, she couldn't write anything inside. Embarrassed, she abandoned it beside her notebook and picked up her plate to stack with his. Her companion was watching her hands.

He must have felt her gaze, because his eyes lifted to meet hers. For the second time that day, planets collided. Perhaps it was as well The Chef With No Name didn't seem inclined to join her team. Love or, worse, lust in the kitchen, were not on her agenda. She hadn't begun a relationship with a colleague since Shaun, and didn't intend doing so now.

Chef looked at his watch. 'I'd better make a move.'

'Will I see you again?' *Did I really just say that? He'll think I'm needy.*

'Excuse me a moment.' He pushed back his chair and stooped, retying the laces of one trainer before standing up. 'That'll depend. I'll have this kit laundered and back by tomorrow morning. Marco's lankier than me but, hey, it did the business.' He held out his hand. 'I'll get changed and use the tradesman's way out. Thanks for lunch, Lucy. I enjoyed working with you.'

Without a backward glance, he left through the saloon doors, or, more accurately, the kitchen entrance. Lucy watched the doors shiver and settle behind him, accompanied by the haunting sounds of spaghetti western music echoing in her head. And when she looked for it, there was no sign of her origami fortune-telling thingy.

4

James lay full-length on his jumbo-sized couch, watching the television news without registering a single fact. He'd sent Dustin a text, asking him to arrange an interview at The Town Mouse without delay. As yet, he'd received no response. Surely Lucy would be falling over her elegant little feet at the prospect of someone qualified stepping in? Especially as she didn't know it was him she'd be interviewing.

Was he utterly bonkers or only slightly silly? She might feel insulted that he hadn't been honest with her. A savvy businesswoman like her would soon suss what his game had been when he arrived, seemingly to try a different eating-place.

Events shouldn't have escalated the way they had. None of his kitchen heroics, no matter how dire the situation. Instead, he should have been in and out of there, and straight off to the agency to talk about the position at the bistro. Lucy would have interviewed him — probably — and he'd have accepted the stop-gap job until the New Year celebrations ceased and the festive decorations fell from their perches.

But now, if Lucy actually agreed to interview James Drummond, the jig would be up the instant he walked into her tiny office. Chefs always got offices the size of a dolls' house. Not that Lucy was very big, he thought, as his mind wandered. He didn't dwarf her, but she was the perfect size to make him feel protective. And as for her hair . . . When she came through to eat lunch, she'd pulled off her hat, mesmerising him with all that blonde loveliness. James groaned. This was no way to begin a professional relationship, however brief it was destined to be.

He yearned to trail his fingers in that hair. He wanted to trace the outline of her sweet mouth before putting his arms around her and kissing her breathless. Boneless. Speechless. All that. He'd definitely lost his reason. Part of him couldn't wait for Dustin or one of his colleagues to contact him. Another part yelled at him to run away from potential trouble.

Why didn't he just take that six-month contract with the big hotel chain? That kind of mission was his forte. The words he'd spoken to Celeste mere hours ago returned to haunt him. *Get in. Revolutionise. Get out*. That tactic was his strength. Different people. Same problems. Relative anonymity.

Like a pilot's logbook clocking up air miles, his CV reflected his experience. What's more, the money the hotel group offered was a whole heap better than a town bistro could afford to pay.

Lucy had offered him the job directly. So why had he dithered, avoiding answering her, before walking away? James knew full well why. The bistro owner had wriggled under his skin, that's why. And he hadn't had the guts to accept her job offer on the spot.

Now, despite the comfortable couch, he was finding it difficult to relax; every nerve in his body was sending potent messages to his poor, deluded brain. Lucy had seemed confident about coping with that evening's bookings. How he hoped her optimism was proved right. For he knew, if he allowed his heart to rule his head, and actually turned up there to check how things were going, he'd probably frighten the daylights out of her, or at the very least, come across as a complete weirdo.

As to what might happen if the agency fixed an interview and she came face to face with the man she already knew as Chef, he really hadn't a clue.

* * *

Lucy entered the kitchen through her private door, wishing she'd slept better. The preceding day's events had proved hard to wash away with half a bottle of white Burgundy followed by hours counting sheep that kept stopping to munch grass. She rarely drank alcohol on a work night, but the emotional backlash of Emily's departure and the stressful luncheon period had played their part in rattling her.

Dustin's phone call, late last night, should have cheered her. Instead, it had only succeeded in making her wish she didn't need to see the applicant he assured her was perfect. Yes, the CV he'd emailed was impressive enough to make her green with envy. But she still wondered about a chef's motives if he was prepared to take second position in the kitchen, knowing he could earn more money, and respect, working at top level.

She mustn't keep thinking of The Chef With No Name, the hero who had burst into her life, stayed a while, and then left again, without even accepting payment. Classic. Also, let's be honest, a little weird. *Forget him, Lucy.*

She sat down, scanning figures while her computer booted up. Yesterday had convinced her, if convincing was necessary, that she'd never handle extra business without suitable help. And that help must start work immediately. That put — she checked the name scribbled on her notepad — James Drummond in pole position. So, provided Mr Drummond seemed competent, clean and tidy, surely she could tolerate him for a month?

Dustin couldn't be holding something back, could he? She already knew James Drummond had taken time out from his busy career. Would this gap impact on his performance?

Lucy checked her watch. The applicant was due in five minutes. She'd be fair and non-judgmental in her assessment of his character, and as to how he'd fit into her team. No, she told herself again. Do not keep hankering after The Chef With No Name! He turned up. But he turned you down.

Like Leanne had said, she needed to

stay positive. Needed to remain calm and cheerful.

Lucy leapt to her feet the instant she heard the doorbell. She dislodged the safety chain, opening up, with a smile on her face. She didn't keep it there long.

'Oh, it's you! I thought it was the chef sent by the agency.'

'Hi.'

Lucy felt anything but calm, positive and cheerful. Had The Chef With No Name, standing there with a black sports bag slung over his shoulder, changed his mind about accepting payment?

'What can I do for you, Chef? If you've had second thoughts over a fee, that's cool, but I have someone coming for a job interview any minute now.'

He shuffled his feet. 'I'm James Drummond.'

'Sorry? Did you just say you're James Drummond?' *Oh gawd, I sound like Great-Aunt Bella in Lady Bracknell mode!*

'That's correct.' He pulled a parcel from his kit bag. 'One chef's uniform, newly laundered. And I owe you an apology, Ms Stephenson. For yesterday.'

She accepted the package. She took in his charcoal grey suit, pristine white shirt and lavender and silver-grey striped tie. He wore shiny black shoes with fashionably narrow tips, so obviously didn't suffer with his feet. Yet. Mentally she ticked off one credit.

'Thanks, although I didn't expect you to deliver this in person, Mr Drummond. Right. I don't have much time and I imagine you understand why. Shall we begin your interview?'

He walked inside. She locked the door behind him. That felt odd. Locking herself inside her restaurant with a strange man. Except he wasn't really, was he? They'd worked together. Pooled their professional skills. High-fived each other after completing the last order. Her head urged her to ask searching questions, but her rebellious body kept saying *Yes. Yes. Yes. Just give him the job. You know you want to.*

'I thought we'd use this table rather than my office.'

He waited until she was seated. 'Where would you like me to sit?'

'Wherever you feel comfortable.'

He pulled out a chair three places along.

'I don't need an apology, Mr Drummond, not after the way you rode to the rescue yesterday. I already know how well you conduct yourself.' *Why do I keep sounding like Great-Aunt Bella?*

'But you do expect an explanation, Ms Stephenson?'

'I do. I don't like time-wasters, Mr Drummond.'

She detected a glimmer of amusement in those deep-brown, velvet eyes.

'Quite right too. Frankly, Ms Stephenson, I'm finding it difficult to understand what happened yesterday, in rational terms, that is. I already explained my first instinct was to offer assistance.'

'Marco was the one who accepted it.' She managed not to let her lips twitch.

'Everything happened in a rush, which is probably what prevented me from accepting your kind offer.'

'I wasn't being kind. I was impressed — by your presentation skills, by your ability to hit the floor running and by your — your compassion.' *Don't go over the top!* 'I merely took the chance to ask if you were willing to accept a temporary position.'

James inclined his head.

'Obviously Dustin explained my situation?' Lucy sat back in her chair.

'He did.'

'So you turned up yesterday, intending to jump straight in?'

'Lord, no! Nothing was further from my mind. It was professional curiosity that sent me here. And having worked with you, I know you'd have coped, even with a reduced staff, if only that hotel hadn't tipped their guests into the street to find food and warmth.'

She did have to smile at that. 'Time of year for it — no room at the inn, and all that! I don't think it was quite as horrendous as some of those guests made out. But, if I might return to the way you responded to my job offer? You still haven't properly explained it.'

He nodded. 'I think my concern was over a knee-jerk reaction.'

'Your knee or mine?'

His turn to smile. 'Both, maybe, if that makes sense?'

'Yes. It does. You might've thought, wow, do I really want to work with a woman who jumps at the first warm, breathing chef who turns up?'

'And you, Ms Stephenson, might have wondered, once the adrenaline rush subsided, what on earth possessed you to offer employment to some guy who literally walked in off the street.'

They stared at each other. 'I need caffeine.' Lucy got up from her seat. 'Would you like a cup?'

He stood too. 'How about I make it

while you decide whether or not to send me away with my tail between my legs?'

Does he realise how cute he looks when he smiles and that dimple pops up . . . ? Enough!

She held out her hand. 'No need. I've already made my decision. Welcome aboard, James, and please call me Lucy outside the kitchen. That is, provided you're happy to accept my second offer of employment.'

She couldn't bear it if he didn't. At this hectic time of year, she'd never find a better chef, or even someone half as good. She already knew this man didn't attend interviews unless he felt the kitchen in question was the right place, which gave her some hope. But the salary she specified must seem like pocket money to a head chef with more experience of feeding the glitterati than anyone else she'd come across.

His CV stated his date of birth and, prior to the interview, Lucy hadn't been able to resist calculating her interviewee's Zodiac sign. James was a Taurus. Last night she'd checked out the typical traits: reliable, generous and loyal. As it turned out, he'd already proved his humane nature. Ambitious — no surprise there. Practical — yes, with an artistic side, of course.

As for sensual — that aspect hadn't bothered her last night, when she still knew the applicant only as a name with a sensational CV. But The Chef With No Name, even at first sight, sent shivers down her spine in an alarmingly delicious way. Those powerful shoulders were part of the package, not to mention his artist's hands. Hands capable of creating edible magic. She closed her mind to the thought of James Drummond's long fingers creating magic away from the kitchen heat.

Why did he still hesitate? Surely he couldn't object to working for a woman? He'd stated his readiness to take a lower grade position, so it couldn't be that, although she must make it clear how much she respected his ability. Convince him two head chefs in one kitchen could work in harmony, especially as he was happy with a four-week contract. Maybe he had something else lined up? Hadn't he mentioned something about having to make decisions before he left yesterday?

'James, please feel free to ask any questions.'

'Nope. I reckon it's a deal, Lucy.'

Then suddenly they were shaking hands and she was asking when he could start, and Lucy wasn't sure whether she felt like time was in slow motion or whether everything was speeded up. She felt excited, exhilarated, anxious and desperate for this to work.

'I can start now,' he said. 'I brought my whites, just in case.'

'That would be an enormous help,' said Lucy. 'As far as I'm concerned, I'd be happy if you moved in here for the next four weeks.'

Lucy felt heat flood her cheeks. She.

Never. Blushed. What possessed her to say something potentially so provocative? With an innuendo like that, he'd think she was propositioning him.

'Only joking!' she babbled, hastily. 'You already know where to get changed.'

He gave her an appraising look. She still wore the skinny blue jeans and pale pink sweater she'd put on at seven a.m.

'I, um, always change for work in my office. I didn't mean you should rush off immediately.'

'Coffee first,' he said. 'While I make it, maybe you could jot down things I need to know? Names and contact numbers of your suppliers. Delivery times. My hours. Stuff like that.'

'Good idea,' said Lucy, sitting down again.

'Oh, and we need to talk about your desserts.'

'My desserts?'

'Yep. Unless you want me to die of boredom while I'm making 'em.'

* * *

'Argh! That man is so arrogant! Believe me, he's more superior than — than a Mother Superior!' Lucy spread her hands. 'Okay, he's good. All right, make that awesome. But doesn't he just know it!'

She shook her head as if to clear it of the irritating subject, and pointed to a whole hake, glistening amongst fractured ice.

'Now, that looks wonderful.'

'Doesn't it?' Celeste Severini clasped her fingerless-gloved hands in front of her red and white striped apron. 'When it's cooked, that hake will be the perfect shade of silver-grey, and you will notice little patches of gold on its gills.'

'James wants scallops too.'

'An excellent choice this time of year. That man's wish is my command.'

'Has my new chef charmed every woman he's met so far in Dexford?'

'Jealous?'

'Me — jealous? Haven't I just been

moaning about him?'

Celeste smirked. Why did an Italian smirk seem so much more crushing?

'Lucy, is this the same guy you told me was an angel in disguise? You couldn't believe someone of his talent was prepared to work in your kitchen?'

Lucy scowled. 'Yeah, okay, point taken. All my staff think James can turn water into wine. But if I gave you his opinion of my dessert menu, you'd understand.'

Celeste chuckled. 'I shall have the opportunity to sample his cooking at the weekend, shan't I?'

Lucy fast-forwarded her brain towards Sunday. 'Of course. I haven't forgotten it's your family lunch party. James muttered something about creating a special dessert. Something to make your heart sing, I think he said.'

'*Che uomo cara*.'

'Sorry?'

'I'm saying what a dear man he is.'

'Right.' Lucy hadn't missed Celeste's

caressing tone. A woman her age should know better.

The stallholder handed over the wicker basket Lucy used for carrying fish. 'It's heavy, Lucy. You should have asked James to make this errand.'

'And have you flirt with him over the fillet of sole?'

The two women exchanged mischievous glances.

Lucy walked the short distance back and went through the rear door, putting down the basket in the delivery area. James sauntered through, an inquisitive expression on his face, and Lucy's stomach performed the usual triple flip she'd come to accept. *Irritating. Going nowhere. Get over it.*

'What did you get?'

'See for yourself.'

James peered into the basket and tore a peephole in the top package. 'Fabulous. Can't wait to have my wicked way with these scallops.'

'And?'

He foraged again. 'This is top quality

hake. Well done, Lucy.'

'Well done Celeste Severini, who, by the way, is a great fan of yours.'

'And of yours.'

'She's known me a while now.'

'That's one of the reasons I want to make Sunday lunch very special.'

Lucy tilted her head to one side. 'You know, you're quite a mystery man.'

'How so?'

'You turn up in Dexford, with a CV lesser mortals would kill for; I'm still wondering why you chose to work at The Town Mouse. And you're treating a local family's Sunday lunch party like it was the Lord Mayor of London's Banquet.'

He shot her a thoughtful look.

'The Severini family is important. Not only as customers but as valued suppliers. They've chosen your restaurant because they trust you to treat them well. What's not to be excited about?' He paused. 'Except perhaps your dessert menu.'

'I thought we'd agreed to differ on

that subject.' She could hear that spaghetti western theme again.

'If I'm employed to help regenerate a restaurant, I refuse to allow any area to under-perform, when, given ingenuity and imagination, it could sparkle. And there's much about your cooking that sparkles.'

He lifted the hake and scallops from the basket.

She folded her arms. 'Thanks, but I have customers who've eaten here for years. They enjoy traditional English desserts like fruit crumble and bread and butter pudding — all the things they remember from childhood. Comfort food, if you like.'

He pulled on a pair of disposable gloves and selected a knife.

'You have a wonderful range of blades.'

'Well at least something finds favour,' she snapped.

'Oh, Lucy, Lucy, there's a lot about you to find favour with.'

Is he flirting with me? Or does he

mean my menus? Minus puddings, of course.

'I'd like to present a selection of four desserts for Sunday lunch. Apart from the Severini booking, it doesn't look like much else is happening.'

'We've had a few cancellations,' she said defensively. 'This is a bad time of year for coughs and colds.'

'Are your people trained to use a little gentle persuasion and encourage the customer to make another booking?'

'We're not selling double glazing,' she said. 'That kind of tactic sounds a little too pushy for my liking.'

'It's not pushy to try and replace a cancelled reservation by reminding your caller of delights to come. And your website isn't seductive enough, in my opinion.'

Lucy counted to ten, silently.

'Emily used to manage the website. I've hardly had time to update it, with all that's been happening.'

'Understood, but I'm here now. Why

don't you let me take over?'

'I'm paying you for your culinary talent. Your cooking skills are incredible.' *There, I've said it out loud*. 'But I don't expect you to annihilate my dessert menu. It's a deal for this Sunday, but don't forget that at Christmas, folk expect traditional, festive fare.'

'Just who do you want to attract?'

I almost said you. How scary is that? Lucy teetered between wanting him to make her decisions and feeling exasperated by his criticisms. She longed for him to help her achieve the bistro's full potential, yet she couldn't quite relinquish control. She knew the areas where the business struggled, but she feared making changes at this emotionally charged time.

'We have a steady lunchtime trade. The other day's takings were well above average.'

He nodded. 'Okay. A one-off overflow from the hotel, so nothing to get excited about. I assume lunchtimes are mainly office workers and shoppers?'

'And older folk who live in the area and come in each week for a pensioners' lunch . . . For goodness' sake, James, why are you rolling your eyes?'

'Lucy, my parents are pensioners, but they don't want the fact rammed down their throats when they're after a tasty, reasonably priced lunch. And there's something else.'

She watched him cut into the hake with awesome precision. He put down the knife.

'You need to increase the price of that seniors' lunch, but I like your Throwback Thursday specialities. Why not encourage your more mature customers to make that the day they come here?'

'But seniors' lunch is every Wednesday.'

'As in, today.'

'Correct.'

'Which means this hake probably won't pull because the majority of your lunch trade expects cottage pie or bangers and mash.'

'People enjoy those things. Expect them.'

'That's why those dishes should be available on Throwback Thursday. Tuesday — your first trading day after Sunday — should attract the young professionals piling in for fantastic pasta or pulled pork or crab cakes — nothing heavy. They don't need to gorge on the sort of food available at the Happy Families' Carvery, or whatever it is down at the crossroads.'

She opened her mouth.

'They need to feel pampered,' said James. 'Cosseted. Most importantly, we need to intrigue them so they can't wait to come and sample the evening delights. And that's not all.'

Lucy glanced at the clock. 'Fascinating as all this is, I do have a restaurant to run.'

'Yes, ma'am. But I'd like a meeting this afternoon.'

'Have you no home to go to?'

His lips curved in a smile. 'The Town

Mouse is my temporary home while I'm under contract. I shan't schlep back to my place after the luncheon service. I shall go for a jog, come back and take a shower, followed by a siesta in the rest room. With your kind permission, of course.'

'We don't have a shower for staff.' She swallowed. 'But you're welcome to use my bathroom.'

5

Lucy sat in her office, wishing for a magic wand. Her figures showed the bad news. She'd been coasting. Not over things like décor and uniforms — every employee who worked front of house looked smart, and kitchen staff dressed appropriately. Clearly the culprit was marketing, or the lack of it.

She'd felt crushed when James Drummond pinpointed flaws after being around only five minutes. What must he think of her business acumen? Not a lot, probably. She'd thrown herself into the annual Christmas bonanza, ignoring all the warning signs. No way was this any fault of Emily's — that situation had just compounded the faults already in existence.

Lucy knew James' suggestions made sense. At lunchtime he'd chalked a blackboard message, announcing the luscious, ocean-fresh hake. They'd sold fifteen portions and he was certain diners would snap up the remainder that evening. He told her she might lose some Tuesday lunch trade but she'd also gain some. There were always people preferring to eat out towards the end of the week.

He'd promised to check out greengrocery prices. She had deliveries arriving each week from three different sources. Why didn't she negotiate a better deal on condition she appointed one of them her exclusive supplier?

'But they're all such lovely people,' she'd protested. 'I've always tried to spread my business around. Aren't we all trying to earn a living?'

'These people won't seem so lovely once you realise what thin ice you're skating on,' he told her.

Lucy knew James was already revitalising The Town Mouse. But, with Christmas fast approaching and so much competition out there, did she expect too much? She'd been congratulating herself on repeat custom from office and shop parties whilst ignoring how forward bookings didn't even come close to last year's.

James bombarded her with suggestions, criticisms and occasional caustic comments. Far worse was the way he bombarded her senses with the sheer impact of his personality. She'd overheard two of her staff discussing him on their break, that morning.

'He looks like a young Steve McQueen.' No mistaking the dreaminess of Leanne's expression.

'Was he hot too?' Vicki asked.

'Just look up *Butch Cassidy and the Sundance Kid* on YouTube.'

Was that the reason why Lucy found it difficult to bond with James? Would she be more receptive to his innovative ideas, if only he was a little more homely-looking? Now that was difficult to imagine!

How she wished she could clock up the same number of meals every day as they'd sold the day he turned up. Her evening trade was patchy but not disastrous. Yet. Even as she thought it, she could imagine how James would respond. He wanted a meeting and this time it wasn't just about the dessert menu. But would her professional pride allow her to confide in a virtual stranger how much fear gnawed at her?

She called up The Town Mouse website. Sucked in her breath when she found no New Year's Eve section. She could have sworn she'd asked Emily to set up a bookings page. If only she'd checked. James Drummond would have.

After Lucy brewed peppermint tea and fixed a snack, she heard the front door open and close. It felt kind of comforting to hear the chef's footsteps cross the restaurant. She looked up at him, noticing how his broad shoulders filled her office doorway.

'Hey, James. If you're hungry, you know to help yourself, right?'

'Yes, sure,' he said. 'I could use a shower first.'

She stared back at him. She'd forgotten her offer.

He cleared his throat. 'If it's still okay, I imagine you'd prefer to point me in the right direction.'

Suddenly, she wished she had the chance to go upstairs and check for stray underwear lurking on the floor. She was meticulous about keeping kitchen clutter to a minimum, but not so fussy about her personal space.

'I'll let you into the flat. When you leave, pull the outer door to, and it'll lock automatically.'

He nodded. 'Excellent.'

He followed her upstairs but, to her relief, while she let herself in, he hovered on the landing. She'd left several bits and pieces airing but nothing too embarrassing.

'Come in,' she said. 'I'll find a bath sheet.'

'I'm sorry to be a pain. I'll bring my own in future, although I promise not to impose on you every single day.'

'It's not as though we'll clash in the

shower,' she said. He didn't laugh. She gabbled on. 'I prefer a nice, relaxing bath myself, but showers are best for a quick sluice.'

Inwardly she cringed. She was digging herself into a hole and her legs had forgotten how to move. He stepped inside. Moved closer. And, for moments, her resolve to remain aloof and professional disintegrated.

'Sorry,' he said, backing off a little. 'I'm probably not too good to be near.'

Lucy found her wits as well as her walking ability. 'I'll fetch a towel. You'll find unisex shower gel and shampoo in the rack. My brother stays here sometimes.'

'I always carry stuff in my kit bag, but thanks anyway.'

He didn't ask what her brother did for a living. Maybe he feared if he showed interest in her personal life, she'd expect him to reciprocate. He could have photographs of his children tucked in his wallet. Probably his wife worked and that was one reason why he didn't choose to travel home between sessions. Lucy suddenly wished she hadn't made it so clear that her brother was the only male visitor who stayed over. How sad was that?

Tough. Stop dreaming about someone you can't have. That was the kind of advice Great-Aunt Bella would dish out, if only she was here and not enjoying retirement in her seaside bungalow. Lucy took a fluffy pink bath sheet from a pile of clean laundry and handed it over.

She left him to it. Shut James inside her flat and set off downstairs. And in no way would she allow her wayward thoughts to conjure up images of what he might look like minus clothes.

* * *

They each headed for the big table. James found that intriguing, as if neither wished to share a table for two, with all the connotations that might involve, despite this being a business discussion.

'If you'd like a beer, you're welcome to one on the house,' said Lucy. 'After that, I'd appreciate your paying for anything you consume — unless it's lime and soda, of course.'

He shook his head. 'I never touch alcohol when I'm working. Afterwards, maybe.'

James wondered how this woman, who didn't realise just how sexy she was, relaxed. He'd hesitated over accepting the job because he found her so attractive. Now, he longed to discover what made her tick, but suspected she preferred him at arm's length. He was, after all, her employee, even though she'd made it clear how much she valued his expertise.

They'd worked so well that first session. Now, Lucy seemed a tad edgy, though that was reasonable given his barrage of suggestions aimed at ramping up trade. This place could be an absolute goldmine. Its high street position was perfect and there was even a multi-storey car park, and a station, all within walking distance.

He got up. 'I fancy a lime juice and soda. Can I tempt you?'

'You go ahead. I'm afloat with peppermint tea.'

'That's an abomination.' He grinned at her.

James, acutely aware of his new boss' gaze following him as he strolled to the bar, glanced her way as he reached for a tumbler. She quickly looked at her notebook. She liked lists. He knew that much about her.

'What's the first item on the agenda?'

He took a swallow of his drink and walked back. She looked so much younger with her golden hair tumbling around her lovely face. How old was she, anyway? Probably not too many years younger than he was. Why no boyfriend on the horizon? He hadn't missed the comment about her brother staying over. She obviously had no style to cramp in that department, unless she preferred to keep her love life to herself. James caught himself. He shouldn't think like this.

He placed his glass on the table and sat down, folding his arms in front of him.

'Lucy, you probably think I'm a complete pain in the posterior, but I truly believe you have a fantastic chance to up your game, while increasing your takings.'

'Thanks. I think. It's obvious I'm underachieving, but I want you to know I'm willing to consider anything.' She clasped her hands in front of her.

He sensed trouble. The kind of trouble he understood. She was close enough for him to reach out and take her hands in his. Would that signify solidarity? Or would such contact light the blue touch paper? Reason said it was much too soon to risk derailing the train before it had hardly left the station.

'Maybe I came over too strong. If so, then I apologise.' He took another swallow of his drink. 'But I have ideas I think are worth trying. Believe me, I like success. I crave work satisfaction. But if you want me to shut up and carve you out a few apple pies and a Black Forest Gateau or three, then so be it. You need only say the word.'

The only sound was a siren shrieking as an emergency vehicle tore down the street. The atmosphere was charged with tension; James squeezed his hands into fists beneath the table so she couldn't see, so hard that his nails bit into his palms.

'I want you . . . ' She faltered.

For moments he thought his heart might stop.

'I want you to guide me the way you think I should go. I realise I've allowed the bistro to sink into a rut. I'm not trying to heap blame on Emily, but she firmly believed in traditional fare, and in many ways that worked.'

James nodded.

'To be fair, she did that kind of thing brilliantly. But she's gone, and I've forced myself to stand back and analyse what's happening. I've an awful feeling it's too late to capitalise on Christmas. I realise we need to stand out from other places offering similar menus, but I've let things slip, James. It's as though I've been sleepwalking.'

'Trust me. I've helped pull round far worse situations than this. We'll make a great team, you and me.'

This time he didn't even consider how she mightn't welcome his touch. He reached out and took her small, rather chilly hands in his big, warm paws and gave them a squeeze. It was, he reckoned, sitting back in his chair again, a brotherly thing to do.

But he couldn't kid himself that his feelings towards this beautiful, annoyingly self-contained woman were anything like brotherly. She mustn't discover how much fire she ignited in him. He'd known rejection and he still smarted. He wasn't ready to feel that way again. If she realised the strength of his feelings, and didn't reciprocate, how would he bear it? How would he bear not seeing her, if she ordered him from her life as swiftly as he'd entered it?

'Let me see how Shaz shapes up,' he said. 'I know she won't be around come spring, but what little I've seen tells me she'll be a quick learner.'

'You and your desserts.'

'I'm afraid so. Marco's keen.'

'Unfortunately, he also has a bad case of hero-worship and that must be irritating.'

'It hasn't escaped my notice. It's nothing I can't handle, so long as he learns and works hard.'

'He will.'

'As for you and me — well, don't you think we should try and recognise what could happen between us, if only we let it?'

He saw a flash of shock in her eyes. Did she, too, feel the electricity he and she sparked?

'I was referring to the way we worked together that first day,' he blurted.

'It was amazing how quickly we

adjusted to each other's working methods,' she said.

He saw her eyes shining. Sensed her longing to prove herself. He needed to stop thinking of her as a woman and keep thinking of her as a protégée. Without muscling in too much. Without letting his defences down so she saw what effect she had on him.

He emptied his glass. 'I'd like us to start a new venture.'

'Surely it's too late? Most people have made their choices.'

He suspected she was struggling not to accuse him of being stark staring bonkers.

'Here's the thing,' she continued. 'We have two separate group bookings expecting the traditional Christmas menu tomorrow, and it's pretty much the same story every evening up to and including Christmas Eve.'

'I didn't mean we should try to persuade people not to eat roast turkey or beef. It's their choice. But will you let me present a taster menu for tomorrow lunchtime, and for any diners turning up without a booking in the evening?'

'A taster menu?'

He nodded. 'Yep.'

'I know it's a popular trend, but I'm not convinced it's right for The Town Mouse.'

'We won't know until we try.'

'How many dishes would you suggest?' She picked up her pen, hand hovering over that notebook she carried round like a comfort blanket.

'Oh, maybe fifty or so!'

'Not funny, Chef.'

'Sorry. How about a maximum of six? Of course, the dishes on offer would depend upon availability of produce.'

She still looked doubtful.

'This kind of menu is fun to do and fun for the customers, Lucy. What's not to like?'

'What would we charge?'

He put his head on one side. 'I guess, for the full selection, we'd charge forty quid. For three dishes, we'd go for twenty-five.'

'So the full selection appears to be a bargain.'

'It doesn't only appear to be, it is.'

'Are these tasters all savoury?'

'Not at all! While we're finding our feet, I'd offer four savoury and two desserts. We'll take baby steps, Lucy. Baby steps.'

'I suppose you know what you're doing, Chef.'

'Once the customers eating turkey see what they're missing, they'll kill to sample the taster menu. You wait and see.'

Lucy was nodding slowly, thoughtfully, then said: 'Oh, I forgot, Dustin's sending a commis chef round tomorrow morning. I'd appreciate it if you sat in.'

'Sure, but you're the one who'll be working with him long term.'

'It's a her not a him,' corrected Lucy.

He wrinkled his nose.

'Surely you don't object to another woman in the kitchen?' she said.

'Of course not. It's your grammar

that's the problem. What's wrong with a she, not a he?'

'Pedant!'

The mischievous glint in her eyes caught him by surprise. Despite his good resolutions, he reached across and ruffled her hair. Saw her mouth open in surprise. James caught himself, and, using every scrap of willpower he possessed, withdrew and folded his arms across his chest.

'So, anyway,' he said, clearing his throat. 'This taster menu. I'm thinking fusion. We need to hit customers with an explosion of flavour. Temperature. Texture. We'll send their taste buds on a sensuous journey, the likes of which they'll never forget. Think crispy, crunchy, soft and melting. Piquant. Creamy. Mandarin and Macadamia — so, Lucy, are you up for it?'

* * *

While James took a nap, Lucy went up to her flat. Walking into the bathroom, she stopped, distracted by that lingering masculine scent. He'd left the place immaculate and she had no doubt her bath sheet would reappear, freshly laundered, like Marco's borrowed togs. The man was a total professional and she should grasp every scrap of advice, each oven-ready suggestion she could, before the day he moved on, leaving her to sink or swim.

She sat down on the side of the tub. He had such enthusiasm. His brown eyes had sparkled as he talked her through his ideas. The last significant man in her life had been a chef too, though not in the same class as James. After Shaun decided to move on, Lucy had vowed never again to become emotionally involved with a colleague. At least he'd given her a couple of weeks' notice. At least he'd worked on through the festive period. Unlike his successor.

But if Em hadn't left, Lucy would never have met James, and if he could help Lucy stay afloat in shark-infested waters, she would be eternally grateful. To do so would prove a tough task, especially as she suspected the recently opened carvery was soaking up some of her former clientele. What did that say about her menu? How on earth could she have become so complacent?

6

Next morning, James let himself in before Lucy came down, this early arrival aimed towards a session fine-tuning The Town Mouse's website.

He'd scrutinised it again and couldn't believe the home page photograph showed the frontage before its makeover. He'd resolved to bring in a camera and take a few views, hoping to jazz up the website. People who hadn't visited the bistro probably thought it looked okay, but he doubted whether its image left them panting to book a table.

He had no quarrel over staff. He'd seen how well the team coped with that manic Tuesday session. He'd learned, during a brief chat with Leanne, that she held a qualification in wine, gastronomy and management. He couldn't believe she was content working away from the London buzz.

'Been there, done that,' she'd said. 'My partner and I have a young daughter and in this trade the hours are odd enough without adding in a London commute. Joel, my other half, works from home two days a week and my mum does the rest. I wouldn't want to rock the boat for the sake of more money and potentially much more job stress.'

'I understand. Plus you all make a great team.'

'I can't recall even one hissy fit and I've worked here for a year. Mind you, it's devastating for Lucy to have a chef walk out like that. I still can't quite believe it.'

'Sometimes, things happen that might seem like the end of the world, but change isn't necessarily bad, especially in this business.'

Leanne had looked sharply at him. 'Funnily enough, when Lucy broke the news. I said to her, stuff happens. I didn't want to start gushing too many sympathetic comments though. One chef down and the other crying into the soup would've been disastrous.'

'Did they make a good team?' he'd asked.

'As far as I could tell, yes.' Leanne had hesitated. 'Maybe I shouldn't say this, but I used to feel Lucy often let Emily have her way over menus. It was as if Emily didn't like change and Lucy went along with that. Perhaps she didn't want confrontation.'

James got up to pour himself coffee. That comment had been enlightening. If he'd identified the root cause of the bistro's apparent success while the takings said otherwise, he must strive to stop Lucy from backtracking, even if his popularity plummeted.

'You're an early bird.'

He looked up. 'Hey, Lucy, why don't you take a look at what I've done so far while I pour you a coffee. I got into the website easily. Your instructions were fine.'

'I'm no technical whiz.'

'Fair enough, but it does concern me

that it's not up to date. What kind of message does that send?'

'Do you mind not jumping down my throat before I've even had breakfast?'

He nodded. 'I apologise. But you know I'm right.'

He watched her sit down and eye the monitor.

He got up and poured her a cup of coffee. 'I brought in croissants. One or two?'

She looked up at him. 'Almond?'

'Yep.'

'You buy my favourite croissants and I'm nasty to you.'

'I'm just as likely to be nasty back.'

She gave him the flicker of a smile.

He moved away. 'Stay there and tell me whether or not you approve of my changes.'

'How many are there?'

'I've set something up so people can reserve tables for New Year's Eve. I'm happy to monitor the system but I need you to check on me — make sure I've asked for all relevant information.'

He left her to it while he placed warm croissants under a napkin in a basket. Found plates and knives. Took them through to the restaurant and chose the nearest table.

She joined him.

'I saved the page; I think you've thought of everything. Thanks, James.'

'My pleasure. I'd hate to work on computers all day though.'

He dipped a teaspoon into a jar of English clover honey.

'I don't even have a New Year's Eve menu planned yet,' said Lucy.

He bit into his croissant, a little stunned by this, but determined not to scold her for not doing her homework.

'Mmm — life suddenly got better,' she said. 'Coffee and croissants are heaven.'

He resisted the urge to pick up a paper napkin and remove a pastry flake from her lower lip. She must have noticed his gaze because she touched her finger to her lip and pushed the fragment into her mouth.

He cleared his throat. 'It's not all bad news, Lucy.'

'I'm sorry for being a misery. It's my own fault I feel like this.'

He raised his eyebrows. 'You didn't cause what's her name to take off.'

'Maybe not, but I took my finger off the pulse.'

'On a scale of one to ten, how bad is the financial situation?' He spoke softly, certain she'd snap at him.

But she gazed at him across the table and gave a little nod. 'I value your interest and I trust you not to gossip.'

'Goes without saying, I'm here to help in any way I can.'

'I'm thinking five out of ten.'

'Ah.'

'If all bookings are honoured, we should break even by the time we reach New Year's Day. If we can somehow attract more business over the Christmas period, I'll be better able to face the January doldrums.'

'Then that's what we do.'

'Excuse me?' She put down her mug.

‘We attract more business.’ He spoke slowly, enunciating each word clearly.
‘Just like that?’
‘No, not just like that. We start our new routines tomorrow. Throwback Thursday’s a great idea, and you say it’s normally your best trading day.’
‘That’s right.’
‘So you play to your strengths. How about some photos to release on social media? I brought my camera with me so I’ll see if Leanne can find a few likely people who’ll agree to be photographed enjoying our food. She can tell them their faces needn’t be shown.’
‘Okay.’
He loved how Lucy’s smile lit up her face, though he hadn’t seen it happen too often so far.
‘And you want to begin the taster menu as from Friday, not wait until Sunday as discussed?’
‘You bet. I’m about to publicise it on the website. Do you have a problem with that?’
She shook her head. This morning,

she'd tied her curls back with a mauve scarf . . . He mentally shook himself and brought his mind back to the matter in hand.

'Good. You can read my suggestions before we save that next section. I'll get a new photo on the home page later.'

She stared at him. 'A new photo?'

He wiped his mouth. 'Don't worry, my friend. I'm not suggesting we upload a line of dancing mice or a picture of your team in fancy dress. The current homepage shows the bistro's former colour scheme. Surely you don't want to keep on living in the past?'

He walked off to put his used crockery into the dishwasher. He knew he'd caught her on the back foot. Again. And she too had her street cred to consider.

She followed him into the kitchen and stood, hands on hips, watching him check out the contents of the big fridge.

'One of us needs to go to market,' she said.

'Sure. How about we put battered

cod on today's menu? With mushy peas, potato wedges and homemade tomato ketchup?'

'Mushy peas? Like you get down the chippy?'

He closed the refrigerator door and smiled at her.

'Ah, Lucy, Lucy, ye of little faith. My mushy peas are nothing like you get down the chippy.'

'How are you going to produce that particular delicacy without having put the peas to soak?'

'I did that last night.'

'Is that so?'

He looked hurt. 'You don't like the idea.'

'It's not that I dislike the idea, James; it's the way you're hijacking my menus.'

'I'm trying to lift you from the doldrums and into the big time. Once you accept your fantastic potential, you'll find life easier. Can you not see that? I wish I knew what else I could do to convince you.'

He moved closer.

* * *

She sensed it before it happened. When he turned to face her, his smile bathed her in warm honey. He must be expecting her to succumb to his brown-eyed gaze. Like the rest of her staff had done!

Sorry James, you're here purely for business purposes. She pushed away a tendril of hair.

'I feel this is a case of running before I can walk.'

'Why so? You hit the ground running a long time ago.'

'Maybe I've fallen at too many hurdles. My lack of experience at running a business shows up now I'm on my own. It's the first time I've been alone at the cliff face.'

She looked down at her shoes. Tried not to let her bottom lip quiver like the wimp she knew she was.

He wrapped his arms around her.

'What on earth do you think you're doing?'

But oh, it felt good, being held again after so long. Especially being held in James Drummond's arms. For a moment, she enjoyed the sensation. Wondered whether to pull away. Or not.

'I'm trying to show you you're no longer alone. And that I know you've had a huge amount to overcome, especially lately.'

It was a brotherly kind of comment, or maybe one a supportive colleague would make. But his voice, deep, calm and velvety, sent tingles from the tips of her toes to the top of her head. She couldn't stop trembling.

'Lucy, Lucy, lovely girl, no way should you be a country mouse. Trust me and I'll help you be so successful, you'll be looking to open a second restaurant before you know it.'

She gasped. His mouth found hers and he was holding her far closer than anyone should hold another person, unless that other person was a lover.

And the kiss went on. And on. She

should stop it. But she didn't want to. Her arms wound themselves around him. But did he feel sorry for her? Was this pity?

Each of them came up for air at the same time. He smoothed that same stray ringlet back from her face and what she read in his eyes was not pity. She saw something she daren't acknowledge because she felt exactly the same emotional mix. And he was a colleague, a no-go area.

'I will, of course, apologise, if that's what you wish.'

Lucy shook her head.

'Alright. For what it's worth, I couldn't bear seeing you look so downhearted, and I very much enjoyed kissing you. But it won't happen again. Onwards and upwards now, okay?'

'Okay.' A whisper.

'Why don't I do the market run? Have you made a list?'

She managed to croak assent. Took the slip of paper from her jeans pocket and handed it over.

'Thanks. I'll be as fast as I can.'

Yes. Because while you're gone, all I'll think about is seeing you walk back in again.

He left. She knew he would collect the basket and shrug his broad shoulders into the navy-blue duffle coat he wore to work. It suited him. She'd teased him about it. Now she wanted to run after him. Snuggle against him. Oh, this was bad. So inappropriate. Although in no way did he deserve any blame. She'd read the signs and, okay, he'd kissed her, but she'd kissed him back. All those hours spent watching Clint Eastwood movies with her mum — it shouldn't have come as a surprise, really.

But her trouble-shooting, golden-fingered chef, having tried to comfort her, had awoken something deep inside her. It would take a huge dollop of willpower to push that feeling back where it belonged.

* * *

Brilliant. Well done, James. How about awarding yourself five stars for tactical expertise? He made his way along the crowded pavements, tempted to use the fish basket as a battering ram to help his progress.

Why had he kissed Lucy? Invaded her space and caught her by surprise? It would serve him right if she rang Dustin to lodge a complaint. It was completely unprofessional behaviour.

But when he'd offered to apologise, she'd clearly indicated it wasn't necessary. Why? He daren't go there. Daren't damage his street cred any more than he already had. He'd spent two months away from the UK. Now he'd accepted a stopgap job, at a ridiculous rate of pay considering what he could command elsewhere. And here he was, behaving like a lovesick adolescent.

James strode through the market hall entrance and looked up at the moon-faced clock. It was only eight a.m. What had happened only minutes before couldn't have lasted long. So why had he lost all sense of time? Not to mention reason. Or, more importantly, forgotten his usual professional conduct.

'Hey, how're you doing?'

James stopped. 'Hello, Mother Christmas.' He grinned at the pretty stallholder. She wore a red and white Santa hat on her cyclamen-coloured hair.

'You really should have one of these, you know.' She gestured to her headgear.

Ah, now that seemed a good way to make amends. He'd buy Santa hats for all Lucy's team. He counted out loud on his fingers. 'Marco, Shaz, Leanne, Vicki, Josh, and Tilly. I'll take six.'

'Fantastic.'

He watched her pick up the hats. 'Better add another two,' he said. Lucy had mentioned someone coming for interview that morning and maybe she'd like one herself.

'I hope one of these is for you,' said the stallholder.

'It wouldn't fit with kitchen hygiene regulations,' he said, deliberately sounding stuffy.

'But it would look great with that duffle coat.' She held a sprig of mistletoe above his head.

'How much do I owe you?' He knew he'd disappointed her.

James paid up and headed for Severini's. Hopefully the pretty stallholder wouldn't think he was too much of a spoilsport. Most of all, he hoped Lucy would accept his gesture in the spirit he meant it.

Celeste spotted him as she finished serving another customer.

'Good morning, James, what can we do for The Town Mouse today?'

'Ciao, Celeste,' he greeted her, adding, 'That's all the Italian I know, I'm afraid. I'm thinking cod fillets. Or fresh haddock, with battering in mind.'

'Now, that's different — for Lucy, I mean.'

He chuckled. 'Yeah. I bet she comes in here soon for a good moan.'

Celeste held up a couple of fillets for his approval. 'You two not hitting it out?'

James smiled at Celeste's version of the saying. 'We do hit it off — most of the time.' He thought of the way Lucy had returned his kiss. 'I'm a bit of a new broom, I'm afraid, but it's all about compromise, isn't it? Could you let me have twenty of those, please?'

Celeste nodded, her hands moving smoothly. 'Lucy will never compromise her standards and I imagine you won't either, so you two should have plenty in common.'

'Maybe.' He shrugged. 'I hardly know her.' He could see Celeste had him sussed. She was looking very sceptical.

'I'd have thought being thrown together as you were would have told you plenty.'

'She told you about that?'

'She was impressed by the way you jumped in at the dead end.'

He hid another smile. 'Any chef

worth his salt would have done the same.'

'I can't wait for Sunday. I say to Lucy how excited I am about our family lunch.'

'Let's hope we can live up to your expectations.'

Celeste went on packaging his purchase. 'Lucy hasn't had an easy time these last couple of years.'

He nodded. 'I only know about the recent disruption.'

'Before Emily, there was Shaun, and that wasn't all roses, trust me.'

'Ah. Now, the way you say that tells me Shaun wasn't just the sous chef.'

'*Precisamente*.'

'Thought so.' He didn't feel comfortable, discussing Lucy's previous love life behind her back. 'Well, I won't be running out on her. She and I share a kitchen. We're not an item.'

Celeste came round the side of the stall to hand over the package. 'Just because you're a hot shot chef, doesn't mean you understand women.'

He burst out laughing. 'I never said I did.' He leaned forward and kissed her cheek. 'Thanks for taking an interest. Now, I'd better go before Alfonso takes his best filleting blade to me.'

* * *

'What do I think about the New Year's Eve menu?' James put a plate of deep-fried battered cod and potato wedges in front of Lucy. 'Help yourself to condiments.'

'This looks delicious. How many did we sell?'

'Fourteen. I've put the remaining ones into the freezer.'

She tapped the batter with one finger. 'Crisp. Good colour.' She flipped it over with her fork. 'No soggy bottom.'

'As if!' He pulled out the chair opposite.

'And the pea puree tastes divine. Hang on . . . ' She helped herself to ketchup and dipped a potato wedge in it. 'I take it all back. This is manna from heaven.'

'It's a traditional British dish treated with the respect it deserves.'

'This is way superior to what most places churn out. I should've known better than to doubt you. Better make sure I can do an equally good job with the batter mix.'

'Marco also should learn the secret. After I leave, it's important you're not the only one who can prepare dishes we've added to your menu.'

She didn't want to think about the time when he wouldn't be around. 'Good thinking. By the way, I must ring Dustin and tell him we both liked Katya.'

'Again, I'm happy to give an opinion but ultimately, you must feel sure she's right. It's no bad thing she and Marco are so close in experience. With any luck, they'll try to outdo one another.'

Lucy swallowed a mouthful. 'Yum. Should we open an upmarket chippy, the pair of us?'

'Sure. We could deep fry candy bars and scandalise the health gurus.'

'You know, I can't help noticing those Americanisms. Have you spent time in the States?'

'I worked in a New York hotel for a year. It should be on my CV.'

She felt her cheeks warm. Of course! She'd noticed a top Manhattan hotel featuring on the glittering CV.

'That must have been quite some experience.'

'In more ways than one. I managed to get myself engaged and married while working over there.'

Lucy reached for her water glass, hoping he wouldn't notice her hand trembling. 'Goodness. A lot happened in the space of twelve months.'

'Yep. And in case you're wondering, I'm no longer married.'

'I'm sorry to hear that.' *Lucy, you are such a liar.*

'Cassie and I turned out to be a disaster. The best thing to come out of our relationship was Sam.'

She watched him attack a large chunk of cod. 'Your son — or is Sam your daughter?'

'Samuel James Drummond, five years of age going on fifteen.'

Lucy laughed. 'I can imagine.' She longed to ask questions but daren't.

'How about you, Lucy? Have you ever been married? I suppose it's rude to ask but it's probably good to know a little of each other's background.'

'I've never been married and I'm permanently single.'

'You mean currently single?'

'If you prefer. Yes, that.' *And likely to be at the rate I'm going.*

'Do you think everyone has a soul mate?'

'No.'

'Nor me.' He rested his cutlery. 'See, I do use a knife sometimes, despite my other Americanisms.'

'I didn't say I disliked them.'

'Why don't you think everyone has a soul mate? Many people do think that.'

'I'm going to finish that ketchup

unless you stop me.'

He picked up the dish. 'All yours, but you only get to empty it if you answer my question.'

She considered. 'I think there are many things to take into account when looking for someone special. Where one lives — how one earns a living. Years ago, our great-grandparents probably met out walking or at a church gathering. My great-aunt met her husband at a Saturday hop in the local rugby club. She always used to say Chubby Checker had a lot to answer for.'

'She sounds fun. Sounds like you're saying it used to be easier for people to get together?'

'Yes, but it's ludicrous to think that going out with Andy from Accounts means he's your soul mate. You get on with him. You fancy him. The relationship deepens. Maybe you decide to marry. Perhaps start a family. But you might've done exactly the same thing had you been able to meet Gary from

Glasgow who's a paramedic or who works on an oil rig.'

'I agree.' He picked up his last potato wedge and stole some ketchup from her plate. 'Chefs work antisocial hours so other folk can socialise. I met my ex-wife at the top of the Empire State Building. I decided I should do some of the touristy things and she happened to be taking her niece out. Back in the day, no way would we have met.'

Lucy wondered who'd made the first move.

'Cassie and I got chatting while Natalie — that's her niece — was taking part in something the Education Centre were organising. We hit it off and somehow we exchanged contact numbers. She knew I was a chef but it didn't put her off.'

Lucy gritted her teeth. *There's a surprise.*

'I didn't want to remain in New York. She was working in HR at the time and managed to get a transfer to the company's London office.'

'Convenient,' said Lucy.

'Yep. At the time it all fit together well. Sam came along two years later but after that, Cassie seemed to pine for her homeland.'

'That's understandable, but tough on you.'

'The fact that I wasn't prepared to make my home in New York must tell you something. If two people really love one another, they'll find a way to be together.' He got to his feet.

'Now, how about I give you a run through of the dishes I want to have ready for tomorrow.'

Lucy focused her thoughts. 'Right. That's not far off now.'

She watched him push open the swing doors and come back, holding a list. 'Here's what I'm planning but feel free to disagree.'

7

'Wow.' Vicki was reading the taster menu choices.

Lucy, with Leanne at the bar, turned around. 'Good?'

'More than good. Is James behind this?'

'Well, yes,' said Lucy. 'We're dipping our toes in the water.'

Vicki giggled. 'Sounds fun. I'll listen out for feedback. Chicken croquettes with red pepper, chard and almond? Sounds divine.'

'We wanted to give the team a tasting session but James is anxious to get on. This menu offers a total change for anyone who turns up wanting a change from Christmas fare. Our traditional menu means a lot to me,' said Lucy, 'but we need to watch trends and choose what we feel's best for The Town Mouse.' She checked her watch.

'I'd better get back. Leanne, I'll leave you to explain about wines.'

She hurried away. The starter menu could have presented a problem regarding the right wine to accompany each dish. But Leanne had suggested she liaise with James to choose a different wine in each case, offering a special rate per glass for diners accepting Chef's choice.

James looked up. 'All well out front?'

'Of course. Vicki's hoping for feedback about the new menu.'

'Let's hope we get chance diners. I firmly believe the tasters, with a larger selection, could be a New Year's Eve money-spinner.'

Lucy opened the big oven, took out a tray of potatoes roasting with herbs and began turning them. 'Now that does sound scary.'

'I don't know why. Think of all those roast dinners at the office party, and at home, and with the in-laws. Then along come turkey sandwiches, curries and whatever else, topped up with mince pies and sausage rolls and frozen chocolate éclairs. Don't you think they'd enjoy the chance to sample something more exotic, without it costing a fortune?'

'Too right! It's a brilliant idea,' said Marco.

James was carving turkey, piling succulent slices on a platter. 'We should get our full selection on the website soon as possible. It's prime party season and important to grab our slice of the pie.'

'Will you still be here after Christmas, Chef?' Marco was looking after a huge pan of cauliflower and Stilton soup.

Lucy turned her attention to a tray of pigs in blankets, crisping nicely and smelling divine. She daren't look at James, but the master chef either hadn't heard above the hubbub or chose not to respond.

Vicki poked her head through. 'First lot arriving. This is the party of twelve, a little early, and Leanne's just accepted a booking for four people wanting to eat at eight-thirty. They'll be on the taster menu.'

Lucy exchanged glances with James. He put his thumb up to Vicki. After that, Lucy forgot everything but the challenge and joy of working in a team and ensuring her customers enjoyed a superb experience.

* * *

'Do you have folks? A mother and father somewhere?'

'And there was me thinking you'd want a forensic examination of tonight's session,' said Lucy.

She and James sat at the communal table, each with a glass of wine and not too large a plate of leftover goodies.

'I'm not displeased.' James held up his glass. 'Your good health. And that of your folks, wherever they are.' He wished she'd answer questions more promptly. Now he was left wondering if he'd put his size elevens in it.

She chinked her glass with his. 'My mum and dad, who live near Reading, were both fine last time I saw them, thank you. As for this evening, it went really well. I just wish we'd done more covers.'

He took a sip of white Bordeaux, chosen by Leanne to accompany the smoked haddock taster. 'What you need is a sandwich board man.'

Lucy almost spluttered. 'Sorry, but isn't that a bit outdated? Do they even exist nowadays?'

'Of course. I think it's definitely worth a try.'

'It just seems a bit, well, tacky.'

'Nonsense. You desperately need to spread the word. How about all those potential customers who never check our website? You should seize the chance to make people aware they needn't drink themselves silly on New Year's Eve to have fun. They can enjoy a relaxed, sociable night while sampling delicious international cuisine.' He wagged a finger. 'Think about it, Lucy.'

'It's all right, you've convinced me — twice, in fact.'

He stared at her. 'Sorry to have banged on unnecessarily but, with the greatest of respect, you're not the best at communicating.'

'Maybe there's a reason for that.'

He gestured to their food. 'Come on, let's eat supper before it's time for breakfast.'

She picked up her fork. He'd told her something of his past and perhaps it was her turn to talk too, though he'd given her an opt-out.

'This haddock smokie is scrumptious.'

'Thank you, ma'am.'

'For your information, I used to be a lot more carefree than I am these days.'

'Hey, you don't need to say anything. I've heard bits and pieces, here and there. I understand.'

There was a brief silence.

'Did you realise you have something of a fan club amongst the team?'

'The one I'd most like to be a

member of has opted out.'

Startled, she picked up her wineglass and sipped.

He groaned. 'That was such a naff thing to say. Do you sometimes wish you could rewind and start again?'

'More times than you'd believe. And I'm often a bag of nerves around you.'

He put down his glass. 'Am I so forbidding?'

'Of course not.' *Get yourself out of this one, Lucy.*

'You're in a difficult position. Everyone's up to high doh over Christmas and you're trying to waltz with your regulars while I pester you to get them into — I don't know — a Flamenco, maybe? No wonder you feel fraught.'

She laughed. 'I should feel insulted, but I see what you mean.'

'And it's not easy, picking up the pieces after people — lovers or friends — walk out.'

'In case you're wondering, I'm over Shaun. I used to share everything with him. Business worries, future plans

— plans for our future, even.'

'And you were let down?'

'I considered inviting him to go into partnership, purely a business venture. I never truly thought he was that special one. It was . . . ' She stared at the Christmas tree, its branches hung with gleaming gold and silver baubles. 'It's taught me to be very careful who I confide in.'

'Then, when Emily arrived, you had a female confidante who was presumably on the same wavelength.'

'In time, yes. She was a good cook, but inclined to prefer the status quo. I think I remained in a kind of limbo, afraid to challenge myself.'

He grimaced. 'Staying in your comfort zone's all very well as long as you fine-tune, introduce subtle changes to cooking methods and combinations.'

She smiled. 'I like the thought of changing my combinations.'

He laughed. 'That's better. Tell me, when did you last go on a date?'

'I beg your pardon?'

'You heard. Finish that wine and I'll pour the next one.'

'As my Great-Aunt Bella might say, are you trying to get me squiffy?'

'No, I'm not, and you really must introduce me to the old girl one day. How many more questions do you intend dodging?'

She watched him fill two fresh glasses, his fingers, as she'd noticed before, long and capable, with well-manicured nails.

'I don't have time for dating,' she said primly. 'Besides, I dislike the thought of joining an online site.'

'You don't attend church gatherings?'

She laughed again. She was starting to relax. 'Not recently.'

'All I can say is, the guys around here must be off their heads. Don't tell me no one's asked you out since Shaun left?'

She shook her head. 'Perhaps I don't send the right signals and, to be fair, how many men actually see me? I come out of my lair to chat up the diners most evenings. But chef's whites are hardly the kind of gear to wear if a girl's on the pull.'

'Will you come out with me on Sunday evening?'

'Whatever for?'

'Well, that went down well.'

'You caught me by surprise.'

'Good. As for why, mainly for fun. Also I think it would be good to go out together. You could put on a pretty dress. I could wear my best duffle coat. Maybe you'd like to eat in the West End? I don't mean somewhere touristy.'

She stared at him. 'I don't understand why you're asking me out, unless you feel sorry for me. There's really no need and anyway, I don't believe in having relationships with my colleagues.'

'Who said anything about having a relationship?'

She knew her cheeks were flushing with embarrassment. 'Ah well, if it's just a fling you're after, don't look my way.'

'You're such a difficult woman. I'm not a long-term colleague so what's the harm in a night out? Also, you'd be doing me a favour.'

'In what way?'

'I might retreat so far into my shell, I'll only leave it for work.' He leaned forward. 'Let's let other people wait on us for a change. Let's eat food neither of us has prepared. Let's laugh and get a bit squiffy. Invite Great-Aunt Bella if you wish, but for Pete's sake, come out with me!'

* * *

James trudged towards the train station, hands stuffed deep inside the pockets of his trusty duffle coat. What a day it had been! Not only did he play his taster menu card, he'd got his way over the New Year's Eve dinner. Next day he'd gather the team and encourage them to use social media. It wasn't his thing but he understood its importance. Marco would jump at the chance and Tilly, glamorous Tills, whose Twitter account was @TillyMouse and who had, to his astonishment, several thousand followers, would surely guide the others.

At least he was keeping busy. He felt a pang. Maybe working on Christmas Day would stop him thinking about Sam. And The Town Mouse reopened for business on 29th December, by which time he hoped his future employment would be fixed.

He arrived at the station and pulled his oyster card from his pocket. Beyond the barrier a rail employee caught his eye. 'Where are you travelling, sir?'

'Earl's Court.'

'I'm afraid that service is suspended. You didn't read the notice?'

'Sorry, but it's been a long day.'

'Your best bet is the bus to Kensington High Street and walk the rest of the way, or get a taxi.'

'Okay; many thanks.' He turned and headed back through the barrier.

Outside, he stopped to think. He was shattered. A bus ride, probably with a drunken chorus for company, didn't appeal. How about he crashed on the rest room couch? He had his own key but he'd need to give Lucy fair warning, as he'd trigger the intruder alarm.

She picked up on the second ring.

'Lucy, it's me, James.'

'Hi, James. Everything okay?'

'I've just found out there's no train. I can't face the bus; would you mind if I spend the night in the rest room? I imagine you'd have to do something clever with the alarm system.'

'I'll sort it. Are you outside?'

'Nope. Walking from the station, so five minutes away.'

She rang off and grabbed her key ring. He couldn't sleep on the staff room couch, he'd freeze. And besides, although he wasn't a giant, he wouldn't be able to stretch out. James could sleep in the second bedroom but how he'd react to that remained to be seen.

She hurried downstairs, let herself in and switched on lights ready to deactivate the alarm. She supposed James would be amused by her pink dressing gown over jimjams patterned with rabbits. *So* not a good look to be caught in, but hopefully he'd just be grateful to be back inside and would hardly notice.

It wasn't long before the doorbell rang.

'Come in. Goodness it's cold out there.'

He stepped inside. 'I'm so sorry to disturb you. I must remember to check the train service next time I have a late night.'

'This is the latest you've stayed and it's my fault.' *I enjoyed sharing supper with you, sharing confidences*. 'The least I can do is offer you a bed.'

'I'll be fine on the couch.'

'I can't let you freeze to death, James! You can use my spare room. I always keep the bed made in case Dan, my brother, turns up.'

'Dan Stephenson? Why do I know that name?'

'Dan's a reporter. A BBC correspondent, I should say. He pops up sometimes on TV or radio — not that I get to see him. Mum usually tells me what he's up to.'

She was very aware of James watching her reset the alarm. Following her across the dimly lit restaurant, out through the kitchen and up the stairs.

Inside her flat, she opened a door.

'Well, this is it. You know where the bathroom is. Through this other door is the sitting room, leading to the kitchenette. Would you like anything to drink?'

He dropped his bag in the doorway. 'No, thanks, I'm ready to crash. You get back to bed, Lucy. I feel terrible about disturbing you.'

'I hadn't actually gone to bed. I'll probably read a while.'

He nodded. 'It's hard to come down after the adrenaline's been flowing.'

'And when you've been talking. I enjoyed talking to you, James.'

He stepped forward. Something in

his eyes made her catch her breath. Had he read something into her invitation to stay in her flat — something she hadn't intended?

He kissed her cheek. She still hadn't responded to his invitation for Sunday night. Her heart thumped and bumped inside her rib cage. She wanted to say she'd like to go out with him but this wasn't the right moment. Despite what he'd said about needing to get away from the bistro, her heart warned her not to become involved. Not to risk falling more deeply in love with him than she already knew she was.

'Sleep tight, Lucy.'

8

She woke next morning, sleep-befuddled, but conscious of bathroom sounds.

James. Hopefully he'd made use of the towelling robe hanging behind his bedroom door. She didn't want to risk encountering a boxer-clad, barefoot chef.

It was still dark. Lucy swung her legs out of bed and tiptoed to her door, peering out. James hadn't left the bathroom so she tiptoed to the tiny kitchen where she splashed cold water on her face. If she made tea, hopefully he'd be back in his bedroom and she could dash to the bathroom.

With a pot brewing, she crossed the sitting room and peered out again.

'Morning,' said a voice, and despite herself, Lucy jumped. James appeared in the spare room doorway, fully dressed.

'You startled me.'

'I didn't mean to. Do you know, that was the best night's sleep I've had in a long time. It's so much quieter here than at my place. The traffic, I mean.'

She needed the bathroom. 'Good. Tea's in the pot. Help yourself. We can fix breakfast downstairs.' *The idea of making toast, rubbing shoulders with you in my tiny kitchenette seems far too intimate.*

'Cheers,' he said. 'What should I do about the bedding?'

'Just leave it. You never know, you might need it another time.'

He grinned. As if he could read her mind and knew she felt she'd sounded a bit forward.

'That's kind but let's hope I don't inconvenience you again. What if Mr Dan Stephenson turned up and found a strange man in his bed?'

Lucy fled.

Downstairs, feeling much more in

command now she wasn't wearing rabbit-patterned pyjamas, she looked around for something light for breakfast.

'Why don't I treat us to pain au chocolat from your favourite bakery?'

'That's a lovely idea.'

'And you can tell me whether our date's on for tomorrow.' He waited a few moments. 'You see? You really are hopeless at answering questions.'

Lucy whirled round. 'You're a fine one to talk! I'd like to come out with you . . . '

'Do I detect a 'but'?'

Melting brown eyes like his should require a licence. She shook her head.

'You didn't let me finish. I'd like to come out with you tomorrow, James. Thank you.'

'Excellent. Now, let's get on with today. I plan to make this restaurant so hot, punters will be fighting their way across London to reach us.'

He was through the door before she could say anything.

Us, he'd said. Us, as in We. Lucy, Lucy, don't start thinking like that. You know it can't come to anything. So don't start remembering that kiss.

* * *

Sunday morning, Lucy was downstairs by seven. This was the day Alfonso and Celeste were bringing their family — children and partners, plus a sprinkling of grandchildren, a total of twenty covers. It should be fun but it would also be demanding, especially as Leanne had taken a number of table bookings, all bar one couple liking the idea of smaller portions and exciting flavours.

James arrived as Lucy was checking the online New Year's Eve Dinner page. He wasn't wearing a duffle coat. Instead he wore a smart black overcoat with a charcoal-grey scarf she'd bet was cashmere. But something else about him had altered.

'Hi.' She gazed at him with a slight

frown. 'I've just realised — you've had your hair cut.'

'I slipped out to the barber's yesterday afternoon. You obviously didn't notice.'

'Sorry, James. You look very, um, different. In a good way,' she added hastily.

'Ha! I thought the curls were becoming unruly.' He did a twirl. 'Isn't this better? More macho?'

She stifled a giggle. 'I truly didn't notice because mostly you were wearing your chef's hat. I expect the girls will miss your curls!'

He groaned. 'Perleeeeese.'

'And you're looking extremely well turned-out for a work day.'

He raised his eyebrows. 'I hope you haven't forgotten our date, Ms Stephenson.'

She swallowed. 'Um, no, Mr Drummond, of course not. I'll have to transform myself after we close. I expect I can find something if I rummage though my wardrobe.'

She omitted to mention she'd tried on four different outfits last night before going to bed. The chosen dress now hung outside the wardrobe, underwear, gossamer tights and high-heeled shoes placed nearby.

'It feels better out there without that icy wind.' He glanced at the clock. 'I'll get changed and perhaps we should make scrambled eggs and toast while we have the chance?'

'Sounds good.' She beckoned. 'Come and have a look at the bookings page before you disappear.'

He walked over to her desk, put one hand on the polished top and leaned in towards her. 'Lovely bit of mahogany.'

'Isn't it? I enjoy looking in second hand shops.'

Close up, he smelled divine. It was that same scent, maybe mimosa or orange flowers but laced with a leathery tang. His hand brushed hers. She didn't move. For moments they kept contact, until he straightened up and she reminded herself they were at work and she must banish thoughts of their date to the back of her mind.

* * *

'They're here.' Vicki burst into the kitchen like a demon king erupting through a trap door.

Lucy looked up. 'I take it you mean the Severini clan?'

'Yep. Why is it Italians are always so lush? It's just not fair. And both those drop-dead gorgeous sons are married.'

James laughed. 'I'm sure there must be some single Italian guys out there somewhere.'

Vicki, looking unconvinced, left the kitchen. James looked at Lucy.

'Ready, Chef?'

'Ready, Chef.'

'Marco, that pile of turkey slices looks about right to me. Good work. I don't think I could have done a better job myself.'

Lucy watched the young chef's face glow with pleasure. James was excellent with her team. Firm, encouraging and equally quick to compliment or to pick up on something not quite right. He had such high standards, you felt like reaching for an oxygen mask in order to match them. There was so much to admire about this man. So much she'd miss when the time came to say goodbye.

On first reading his CV, she'd wondered what would tempt him to work alongside a small-town chef in a bistro that didn't exactly attract the smart set. While Dexford possessed many attributes, none of its restaurants were awarded a Michelin star. Now, she dared hope The Town Mouse punched above its weight, with the kind of food Lucy hadn't even thought about offering until James opened her eyes to a whole new world. Maybe she'd get the nerve up to ask him why he hadn't taken a better offer, when they were alone together in whatever venue James chose for their date. She felt a shiver of anticipation.

In the restaurant, drinks were being served. Front of house staff were wearing their Santa hats. Alfonso and Celeste had selected the wines up front. Each family member had made his or her food choices. This signposted a routine production for the staff and here was the star chef, handing over more responsibility to Marco. Lucy approved. And what's more, she didn't feel in the least sidelined.

Marco and Shaz were practically running the Severini show. Which was good, given the arrival of several groups yet to choose from the options chalked on the board.

Vicki was back soon. 'Four of each savoury,' she said. 'These people told me they skipped breakfast so they can go right through the menu.'

'Excellent. They know about the house choice of wines?' asked James.

'Yes, Chef.'

James was dipping cauliflower florets and prawns in batter and deep-frying them. Lucy was arranging glossy sprigs of watercress on white plates with one hand, stirring creamy fudge sauce with the other.

'So, Lucy — when the Severini clan finish their first course, why don't you go chat to them? It'll bring home to them how much you value their custom as well as their top quality produce. They'll feel special.'

Lucy stared at James. 'I usually go through towards the end.'

'I know.' He grinned.

'What?'

He shook his head.

'Ah, this is about me and my rut, isn't it? Okay, Chef, I'll show you I can do impromptu.'

She waited until a convenient point before heading through to front of house. Alfonso spotted her as she approached the large tables the staff had arranged into a T-shape.

'*Dolce signora*,' he called. 'Come and meet everyone.'

'I know some of you already!' Lucy smiled at the couple's twin daughters, teenagers now, and each probably petrified she'd tell everyone how she used to babysit them.

Lucy moved round, and whispered between the two girls' glossy dark heads, 'You both look so cool in those outfits.'

Celeste beamed with pride. 'We are having such a lovely time, Lucy. And so far, everything has been perfect.'

'Ah, you've only had one course,' Lucy teased. 'And if you'll excuse me, I'd better get back or I'll be out of a job. There's a very strict chef back there, believe me.'

Celeste gave her a very strange look. On the way back, stopping for a quick word with other patrons, Lucy couldn't help wonder whether James had mentioned their date that evening to the woman upon whose shoulder many people cried. Lucy decided the next chance she got, she would clarify to Celeste that this outing was all about bonding, providing an opportunity to discuss Lucy's business, while relaxing away from it.

* * *

When the customers had left and everything was refrigerated or locked away, Lucy felt as if she was about to play truant. She ignored this oddly exciting feeling and gathered her team as usual, to thank them for their efforts and remind them everyone's share of the tips would be ready when they next arrived for work.

Today, she was acutely conscious of James standing patiently by. When she finished, she looked at him.

'James, I wonder if you'd like to add anything. Any thoughts on your time with us so far?'

He nodded, face expressionless. Her tummy lurched. Would he pick holes in the service? Reveal some awful discrepancy she hadn't noticed?

James cast his gaze round the assembled staff.

'Between you and me, during my

career, I've worked in one or two rather smart watering holes.'

He paused while a nervous ripple of laughter ran round.

'I've encountered plenty of big egos. I've sometimes needed to watch my back. But here?' And then a smile lit up his face. 'Here, I've received nothing but generosity and kindness. What a great team you guys make! You're such a supportive group, in both the kitchen and front of house. Yesterday, I forgot to add a vital ingredient to a particular dish. Marco noticed and without saying a word, placed the forgotten spice in front of me and went about his business.'

Lucy watched her team looking pleased at the praise. Someone started clapping. Marco, cheeks scarlet, looked as though he'd scored a five-star review.

'I'm thoroughly enjoying working with you all.' James turned to Lucy and the moment those brown eyes met hers, her knees and spine went into melt-down. *Get a grip!*

'Lucy, I'd like to thank you for allowing me into your kitchen. Everywhere I work, I learn something different. Maybe it's about a local delicacy, or a technique I decide to steal! Often I learn something about human nature. And that brings me to the awesome level of commitment and loyalty shown by every staff member at The Town Mouse.' He folded his arms. 'But that's enough of my ramblings. Enjoy your time off and let's see if next week we can do more covers than we did this one. Don't forget to do your stuff on social media. Just because I'm an old fuddy-duddy doesn't mean you should follow in my footsteps.'

Lucy chipped in. 'James, I think we should mention your sandwich board man suggestion, don't you?'

He shot her a pleased look. 'Okay, everyone — if you know someone who'd like to earn some cash, spreading the word about our fantastic food and sparkling Christmas offers, please let us know. It can be a student or a pensioner, anyone who doesn't mind parading around with a board.'

After her team trooped out, Lucy locked the door and walked towards James, who was downing a pint of water.

'That was kind, what you said. Thank you.'

'My pleasure — they deserve praise. If I'd noticed anyone not keeping up, I'd have told you quietly so you could deal with the matter in private.'

She nodded.

'I'm delighted you've opted to give my advertising idea a go. Shaz thinks her younger brother would be up for it. She'll text you.'

'Brilliant.'

'So when will you be ready?'

Lucy hesitated. 'I'd love a shower.'

'You and me both.'

She stared at him. 'Um, I'm sure we have time for both of us to use the bathroom. 'You go first, James, while I check I've done everything.'

'Would you like something to eat or can you wait?'

‘What time were you planning to have dinner?’

He looked at his watch. ‘Probably sevenish, by the time we’ve finished here, got to town and gone for a drink.’

‘So, maybe a little bread and some of that delicious pâté?’

‘Great. When we’re on the train, I’ll ring the restaurant. It’s just off Kensington High Street. Afterwards, we could see a movie, if that appeals.’

Sitting beside you in the darkness? ‘Let’s see how we go.’

‘I’ll fix a snack while you do your checks. You’re only allowed five minutes though, Lucy.’

* * *

While James took his shower, Lucy, still unsure what to wear, took a red dress from its hanger and held it against herself. Again. Although tempted to settle for a favourite black — safe and flattering — visions of the red dress had tantalised her.

If the old favourite represented the tried and tested, the red seemed symbolic of a new lifestyle, one that included success. Lucy, not daring to hope for more, pushed the black dress back in the wardrobe. The man she was going out with, on a proper date, as he insisted, wouldn't know what a turning point this colour choice was. If red signalled danger, so be it.

Lucy heard James call out that he'd finished. Afterwards she would recollect that afternoon's shower and hair wash as the speediest she'd ever achieved. Back in her bedroom she towelled her hair before blow-drying, making a face at herself in the mirror as the curls spiralled in their usual relentless way.

'Oh, for straight hair,' she sighed.

She couldn't for the life of her imagine why she put on the expensive lingerie her mother had bought her for her birthday, only for it to languish in her top drawer ever since. Maybe the red dress deserved the best.

The slinky garment slipped over her

shoulders and down her body, settling round her shape like cling film. It hugged her hips and ended just below the knee. She'd scooped up her blonde curls, allowing a tendril to escape either side of her head and her black high-heeled shoes lent her legs a bit of oomph.

Lucy sprayed a generous whoosh of perfume upwards, letting it drift into her hair. Kiss her skin. She collected her black winter coat, a scarf to match her dress, and her handbag.

The guestroom door stood half open. James must be in the living room, or in the restaurant. Calling his name and receiving no response, she locked up and headed downstairs. What if he'd changed his mind? She didn't think she could bear it if he had.

9

He stood at the front of the restaurant, against the bistro's wide window, an unmistakeably masculine figure in the half-light.

Her high heels clicked against the pine flooring and James turned around.

She stepped on to the carpeted area.

'You look stunning,' he said.

She sucked in her breath. 'Dim lighting always flatters,' she said, brushing off the compliment, trying not to show how it had touched her.

'Lucy, Lucy,' he said. 'Let's go. You deserve to be shown off.'

He hoisted his bag over his shoulder. 'I can drop this off at mine on the way to the restaurant. It won't take a minute.'

She activated the alarm. They stepped outside and she locked the door. Silver fairy lights, draped inside the window, twinkled and winked.

He took her hand and tucked it inside his elbow so they walked down the pavement to the station as a couple. Lucy felt protected. And a little excited. And edgy. All at the same time. It was ages since she'd gone out with a man. She and Shaun hadn't had any date nights since that one-off Mediterranean holiday. Looking back, she marvelled at how she could have tolerated a relationship that seemed to revolve only around her business.

She wondered what working with James would be like after they'd crossed this boundary, venturing into the world beyond the bistro — into her life. Was this evening a mistake?

James looked up at the sky. 'I wouldn't be surprised if it snowed.'

'Oh no,' she wailed. 'I should've worn boots.'

'I am so glad you didn't.' His voice sounded husky. She felt his biceps flex beneath her fingertips. She was turning into marshmallow and there was nothing she could do about it.

* * *

Outside Earl's Court Tube Station he hailed a taxi, giving the driver an address she couldn't hear. True to his word, James jumped from the cab, disappeared down a flight of steps off the forecourt of a substantial-looking house, and reappeared a couple of minutes later.

'How long have you lived here?' Lucy asked as the cabbie pulled away.

'A couple of years. I rent the garden flat. It suits me; not that I'm there much, except to sleep. I should buy my own place, I suppose.'

'You probably travel a lot,' she said.

'I look out for jobs in London, mostly. Hopefully, when Sam's a bit older, he can spend part of his summer holidays with me.'

'You'll enjoy showing him all the sights,' she said.

Maybe this explained why he'd opted

to work at The Town Mouse. A short-term contract allowed time for him to consider his options in the New Year, plus he didn't face a long commute.

Lucy felt as though they were both on their best behaviour, and not entirely relaxed. Since he'd commented on her appearance and after the little show of affection while walking to the station, he seemed to have withdrawn. Maybe he was regretting his invitation. Maybe he wished he'd been able to lock his door behind him and settle down with a DVD and a decent bottle of wine.

'Lucy,' he said. He reached across and squeezed her hands. 'Here we are, acting like tongue-tied teenagers. How sad is that? What should we do about it?'

For one wild moment she contemplated kissing him. The cab driver was waiting for traffic lights to change. The first notes of *Driving Home for Christmas* filtered from the sound system. But a kiss would send a message very contradictory to her feelings about romantic entanglements with work colleagues.

'Talk about the weather?'

'Let's ask our driver what he thinks.' James leaned forward. 'Hey, mate, do you reckon it'll snow tonight?'

'Nah, no chance,' said the cabbie.

'Thank goodness,' said Lucy as the traffic lights changed and their driver took an immediate left turn.

'I've asked him to drop us at the Beaufort for drinks first.' James reached for his wallet. 'Here we are.'

Inside the bijou hotel, Lucy enjoyed the feel of luxurious carpet beneath her feet as James steered her into the cocktail bar. A waiter showed them to a table for two and pulled out a chair for her.

'May I take your coat, madam? Sir?'

He glided away, leaving elaborate drinks menus on the table.

'These are almost as big as sandwich boards,' said James.

'So they are!' She wondered whether he felt more comfortable talking shop. Here with him, out of her comfort zone, she couldn't help think what a strange situation they were in. Neither of them was looking for a relationship. There really was no urge to impress. He'd seen her, pink-cheeked and perspiring, stirring simmering soups. She'd seen him gutting fish, flinging bones in the bin.

Kitchen conversation reflected timing and presentation, each of them striving to co-ordinate with the other while overseeing their team. Unable to relax in these luxurious surroundings, she suspected James felt the same.

'I'm hopeless at choosing.' Lucy scanned familiar and bizarre names and descriptions.

'How about a Cosmopolitan?' He leaned across to point it out on the menu.

'It sounds fairly lethal, James. Maybe a Bellini's more my style.'

James caught their waiter's eye and

ordered Lucy's drink plus a whisky sour.

'Tell me about your son,' she said.

His eyes shone. 'Sam's scarily mature in some ways yet reassuringly fond of doing the things little boys should do.'

'I don't have much to do with young children,' Lucy admitted. 'When I used to babysit Celeste's twins, they ran rings round me on the family computer.'

'Tell me about it. Sam's like lightning, using a tablet.'

'But think of all the skills you possess. When he's older, he'll appreciate how much his dad knows.'

'Maybe. Nice of you to say so.'

He looks a little pensive. Change the subject!

To her relief, their cocktails arrived. After the waiter retreated, James raised his glass.

'Here's to The Town Mouse.'

'I'll drink to that,' she said. 'But I'd like to toast whatever project you take on when you leave us.'

His smile was wry. ‘Long way to go yet, Lucy.’

They drank in silence. She was unsure whether he sounded resentful or resigned.

The cocktail helped her unwind. Before long, she was telling him about her cookery course, a career choice her father hadn’t totally approved of.

‘He wanted me to become a teacher,’ she said.

‘Maybe you will, some day. Teach others to cook, once you hang up your chef’s hat.’

‘Life after The Town Mouse isn’t something I think about.’

‘Quite right too,’ he said. ‘Now drink up and we’ll move on. I hope you’ll approve of my choice.’

* * *

She approved all right. At first she’d considered its name, A Kitchen, to be a little strange, and hoped the chef didn’t try to be too clever. But she didn’t think James would bring her here if that were the case. Its minimalist décor intrigued her and the quirky food descriptions made her laugh.

'Broken Egg Omelette served with apologies,' she read aloud.

'It's a favourite of mine,' said James, 'but how about a starter?'

She hesitated. 'I do so love desserts. Not sure I can go three courses though.'

'Now you see why I'm so keen to promote the taster menu for the bistro. How about we share a dish of olives? Maybe order their not for the faint-hearted Guacamole, prepared at the table and served with nachos?'

He guided her through the menu and ordered a bottle of white wine, despite her protests about walking back.

'Nonsense,' he said. 'Leave me to sort it out.'

While they waited for their main courses she glanced through the window. An urban garden had been created, giving the opportunity to dine al fresco. Fairy lights shimmered on a huge fir tree in the middle of the patio. Lucy looked more closely; sure enough, tiny fragile flakes had started to float down, settling like sequins on paving stones and table tops.

She was about to point this out when she realised James was getting to his feet.

'Sorry. I'll be right back,' he said, before moving swiftly away.

* * *

James found himself between a rock and a hard place where Lucy Stephenson was concerned. He'd begun their acquaintance by feeling sorry for her, so badly let down at the peak time of year. He'd decided to accept her job offer, despite its less than attractive salary, and despite the fact that Lucy traded in suburbia, in an area where most chefs of his calibre would never dream of working.

He'd asked himself what he thought

he was doing ever since. Especially after he kissed her. She'd felt so right, so perfect, snuggled against him, arms holding him as firmly as his held her. Her lips soft and giving beneath his.

How could he explain, even to himself, the difference in the way he'd fallen for his former wife and the way he felt about this blonde enigma? Lucy had stormed her way into his heart and stolen his reason, all the time making it clear as metre-high capital letters how much she scorned relationships with colleagues. She was enthusiastic, passionate even, about her business but equally, she could be lukewarm about change. But there'd been nothing lukewarm about their kiss.

In the washroom he rinsed his hands. Turned on the cold tap and bathed his face. To a casual observer, he might look like a man feeling the effects of alcohol, but that wasn't so. He was feeling the effects of Lucy.

Yet he knew every day that passed brought him a day closer to the point where contact with her ceased. If he could only rein in his emotions until his contract ended, he'd be in a position to ask her out on a proper date. Not a half-baked attempt like tonight's dinner, which he'd thought might be a friendly gesture, given how hard she worked. But he longed to romance her. Longed to take their relationship one step further. Right now, though, with Christmas up close, was not the time to distract her.

James left the washroom and headed back to find Lucy gazing through the window, elbow propped on the table and her chin resting in her hand. Did she have any idea how he felt? Would it be so very terrible to kiss her once they got outside? After all, if she returned the kiss as warmly as that first time, wouldn't that prove something special existed between them?

At present, neither he nor she had much idea of how to navigate the evening.

'Penny for 'em.' He pulled out his

chair and smiled as she turned to face him.

'I'm sorry, James, but I really think I should make tracks for home.'

10

James followed her gaze and took in the thin, white layer already covering the ground. Whirling snow crystals were spotlighted like theatrical special effects.

'It's got worse in the last few minutes,' she said.

He sighed. Snuggled up in a log cabin, feathery white crystals falling from the sky would spell romance. But tonight? He thought quickly.

'Whether you go now or later, Lucy, I shan't let you travel back on your own. But the next course is on its way and I have a much better idea than cutting short this delicious dinner.'

'I'm listening.'

'Why not come back to my place?'

At that moment, their waiter returned. James imagined Lucy would be grateful for the chance to consider his invitation. He said nothing until their waiter deployed a black pepper grinder the size of the Eiffel Tower, wished them *bon appétit*, and left.

'It makes sense, Lucy,' he continued. 'There'll be a normal train service tomorrow and I can drive you to the station early if you don't fancy a lie-in.'

'I didn't know you had a car.'

'I hardly ever use it while I'm working in Dexford.'

'I still think I should go back tonight.' She looked down at her plate. 'This is awesome, but if I skip dessert and coffee, I can make the nine-thirty train and be out of your hair.'

He sighed. 'If you insist, but I'm definitely coming back with you.'

'But why would you bother?'

He shook his head. 'For goodness' sake, I won't allow you to travel alone on a late night train. Who knows what kind of drunken yobs might be around? Don't even think about it.'

'Please don't fuss.'

'I'm merely stating a fact.'

'But it's such a waste of time.'

'Maybe. But you won't accept the alternative.'

'I don't even have a toothbrush.'

'You think I don't keep a drawer of essentials in case I have an overnight guest?'

Watching her uncertainty, he felt a surge of tenderness. She was such a mixture of vulnerability and pig-headedness.

'Lucy, Lucy,' he said. 'I'm not into one-night stands, which makes two of us, right? All I'm offering is a bed and some toiletries — a morning cuppa, even, before you take the train.'

'What if there's a whiteout?'

'We're in London, not North America, so I think you're probably safe. I guarantee you won't be attacked by hungry grizzly bears.'

'I'm being silly, aren't I?'

'You've gotten used to looking out for yourself. Nothing silly about that.'

She noted the Americanism. Shades of Cassie and his time in the States.

Despite what he'd said, was he hankering after family life?

'Does your ex-wife ever stay with you and bring Sam?'

He shook his head. 'No, it's easier for me to be the one to visit them. Cassie hasn't crossed the Pond since she moved back to New York for good. Like yours, my guest room is sought after by a family member, in my case a twenty-year-old niece, studying at Reading Uni. Evie likes the theatre, and her Uncle James' accommodation is free. As she's incredibly scatty, she often forgets her toothbrush, though she's been known to turn up with a mate in tow, which is why I keep a futon in the second bedroom.'

'You know,' said Lucy, 'I might just find room for a dessert.'

* * *

'It's probably quicker to walk,' he said as they put on coats. 'Our waiter says there's a fifteen-minute wait for a taxi.'

‘Let’s walk then.’ Lucy was wrapping her scarf around her neck.

He opened the door. ‘Grab hold of me so we can fall down together.’

‘What in the world possessed me to wear high heels?’ She squealed as one foot slid beneath her.

But James had her in his grip and pulled her close. ‘Let’s try to get back in one piece. A lot of folk expect you to cook their dinners between now and Christmas, and that wouldn’t be easy, hopping round in a plaster cast.’

‘Good point.’ The cold air was so sharp their breath made white puffs in the air.

‘Once we get off the main drag we can walk in the road, and by the way, you look beautiful with snowflakes in your hair.’

She almost batted away the compliment but instead looked up at him. ‘What a lovely thing to say.’

They walked on in silence until he guided her around a corner and she recognised the small park across the road.

'This looks a great place to live.'

'Yep. They have a giant chess set too.'

'I can play chess,' she said. 'I'm not a whiz, but I do get it.'

'Don't tell me — Great-Aunt Bella taught you!'

She laughed out loud. 'How did you guess?'

'We're here.' He opened a wrought iron gate. 'I'll go down just ahead of you. Better hold tight to me as well as the handrail.'

At the bottom she breathed a sigh of relief. He opened the door, reached inside and flicked a switch. 'You go first and I'll lock up.'

When he turned to face her, she saw snow lodged on his hair like frosting on a cake. She sucked in her breath, the longing for him to kiss her counterbalanced by apprehension. How might a brief fling, however tempting, affect their working relationship?

When he'd mentioned keeping items for overnight guests to use, a surge of something so strong had hit her, she couldn't at first place it. It had stung. *Lucy Stephenson, you're jealous of any other woman who might have gone home with him.*

They stood facing each other, standing slightly too close.

'Two people who don't approve of one night stands,' she reminded him, softly.

He nodded. 'Clearly a send in the clowns moment. Difficult to know what to say.'

She nodded.

'Let me help you out of your coat and show you your room,' he said. 'Evie keeps a spare hair dryer and a towelling robe in there. Don't forget to switch on the electric blanket, so you'll be nice and toasty.'

It's better like this. James is a gentleman. He wouldn't dream of behaving in any other way.

But by the time she was ready to

douse the bedside light, she was convinced she'd either missed a golden opportunity to accept a few sweet weeks of happiness, or else James viewed her as nothing more than a friend, and his compliments resulted from Christmas cheer. She'd never felt so lonely in her life.

* * *

Days hurtled by. James turned up early the following Tuesday. Polite. Professional. Purposeful. Lucy was the one with the jitters, not daring to confess how she'd spent most of the night hours wondering and worrying. All right, panicking.

'You look pale, Lucy.' At market, Celeste's gaze was searching when Lucy turned up with her basket.

'There's a lot to think about, this time of year.'

'But you have such a wonderful team. You know, that lunch we had was out of this world. The panna cotta with strawberry and rhubarb compote was to die for.'

'That's lovely to hear. James wanted it — *we* wanted it — to be, you know, a bit special.'

'You succeeded.' Celeste bagged up smoked haddock fillets. 'That's a lovely man you have there, *cara*. Don't keep him at arm's length. Life is too short for dangling.'

'Um, do you mean dawdling?'

'You know what I mean.' Celeste shot her a dirty look. 'He can't take his eyes off you.'

'Oh, I think he can! Otherwise there'd be chaos in the kitchen.'

'Open your own eyes, Lucy.' Celeste followed up with a rapid flow of Italian. The only word Lucy even remotely recognised was *idiota*, which was maybe as well.

She left, wondering what she was supposed to do. They were counting down the days to Christmas. She desperately needed her takings to top last year's. James was pledged to help her. Neither of them had time for romance, even if Lucy had been convinced James was ready for a new relationship.

Their sandwich board man arrived soon after Lucy got back. James dealt with him.

'How did you conjure up those boards, let alone transport them?' she quizzed him, after the man set off.

James tapped the side of his nose. 'I have contacts. And a car, remember?'

He asked if she'd mind him working with Shaz on desserts. 'I'd like you to see how Marco operates now I've fine-tuned a few blips.'

She felt numb, but pleased. Maybe she wouldn't need to interview for a new sous chef after Christmas. Maybe Marco could step up to the plate in more ways than one.

'Fine by me.'

Lunchtime trade was brisk, verging on amazing for a Tuesday. Afterwards, James excused himself and left without lunch, saying he'd be back by five. Lucy made a sandwich and ate it, glued to her computer.

And so they continued for the rest of that week. Each day, Lucy watched her takings soar as her mood plummeted. Although she felt she could hide her feelings well enough to fool her staff, she asked James to take over the fish run, fearing further comment from Celeste might tip her into tearfulness.

Lucy missed those snatched suppers, impromptu breakfasts and the way they'd begun learning each other's ways. She'd blown it. And on the Sunday, as soon as they closed, James told her he was off to spend the night with his folks.

'Enjoy yourself,' she said, walking him to the door.

'Thank you. You know, you should fit in a visit to your parents. Unless you're going there Christmas Day,' he said.

'No. I mean, yes I know I should, because I'm not spending Christmas Day with them. I'll probably be shattered, so we've arranged for me to see them on Boxing Day.'

He nodded. Then he was gone, walking briskly to the multi-storey car park, she supposed.

* * *

By the Sunday before Christmas, she decided she could stand no more.

'James, could you stay for lunch today, please? I'd like to share some information, but as we're open tomorrow, this is probably the best chance we'll have to talk.'

To her relief, he agreed.

'Can do. Cassoulet's finished but there's steak and mushroom pie.'

While he served their meals, she walked down to the bar and selected a bottle of wine, uncorking it and collecting two glasses.

'I hope you're not driving today?'

'I'll be taking the train. No sandwich boards to transport.' A glimmer of a smile lit his face.

'Which were such a success. Still are

a success, judging by our takings.'

'I was hoping you'd say that.' He accepted a glass of wine. 'Cheers, Lucy. Here's to changed fortunes.'

She looked at him. 'You've been keeping yourself to yourself.'

'Not at all. I'm determined that when I leave, your staff will be more savvy, more confident than when I arrived.'

He's deliberately misunderstanding.

'I really do appreciate all you're doing. Now, remember when you said to me that one day I might be considering opening another restaurant?'

'I do, but you shouldn't bank on the New Year being full of good cheer. January's traditionally a month of belt-tightening.'

She nodded. 'I know that. But I've learnt from the local paper that the shop next door's closing down, so the lease is up for grabs. I just wondered what you thought. Wondered whether you'd advise my talking to my bank. Or is it too risky a proposition?'

He swallowed a mouthful of wine. 'Mmm, you have a good house red. There're a lot of positive things happening around you, Lucy, but I'm not sure I'm the right person to advise you right now.'

She bit her lip. Her chest felt tight. Was he going to distance himself from her for the remaining time of his contract? Could she bear it? Did she wish he'd walk out of her life as suddenly as he parachuted into it? If he did, though, she knew she would be devastated.

'I'm sorry if you feel I'm imposing on your generosity,' she said.

He put down his fork. Pushed back his chair.

'I wish you wouldn't be so — so hesitant.'

'Me? Hesitant? I've just asked your advice on a business venture. Hardly hesitant behaviour, I fancy.' She pushed back her own chair and stood, facing him, determined he shouldn't look down on her; well, not too far down on her, anyway.

'Lucy, Lucy,' he said, shaking his head. He sighed.

'I will honour my contract, Lucy, but agreeing to have lunch with you today was a mistake. I'm sorry. I think I've been fooling myself things could be different. Obviously I'm wrong. I apologise if I've caused you any distress.'

He turned and headed off, she guessed to get changed before leaving. He'd honour his contract, of course he would. But what was that stuff he said about fooling himself things could be different? He must have decided she wasn't capable of expanding The Town Mouse. He hadn't even allowed her to share her ideas — ideas that had helped keep her sane every day since that strange, mishandled date that clearly wasn't a date.

Lucy took the half-full bottle back to the bar and fitted a wine saver. She cleared away their half-eaten meals and took the dishes to the kitchen. She had her back towards James when he came in.

'I'll see you tomorrow. Enjoy the rest of your day, Lucy.'

'Yep. You too, James.'

And then he was gone, out of there, the sound of his booted feet stalking across the pine flooring echoing in her head. If he'd been wearing spurs, they'd have been jingling.

Lucy heard him close the door.

That was it then. She needed to forget any idea that James might've been interested in going into business with her. Instead, she'd need to rattle Dustin's cage regarding a permanent chef to begin work in January. She walked slowly across the deserted restaurant and saw James had fetched in the blackboard with those tempting food items chalked upon it. And suddenly, she knew what she must do.

11

Lucy double-checked everything. Stowed. Stacked. Refrigerated. She ran hot water over their barely-used plates. Set the answer phone and let herself out, racing upstairs and rushing into her bedroom, tearing off her whites, wondering what to wear. She pulled on her favourite blue jeans. Rifled through her sweater collection and selected the pale-pink, fluffy sweater she'd been wearing the day he came back to be interviewed. He'd given the outfit a very significant look, and she had felt a tiny, warm glow, even though she dismissed it at the time.

Lucy dressed at a speed appropriate for someone vacating a burning building. She pulled on black suede ankle boots. Reached for a parka with a fur-lined hood. Let it snow, let it snow, let it snow — she couldn't care less. Not that there was much chance of that, given the last lot had swiftly melted into slush.

She'd kept the toothbrush borrowed that night when James convinced her not to cut their evening short. Now, she shoved it into her handbag, along with a brand new one she kept meaning to hand to him. Well, the time had come, and although she hadn't a clue when the next train to London left, she intended being on it. The thought of not seeing him until he turned up for work the next day filled her with a mix of despair and intense frustration.

What if he thinks you're throwing yourself at him?

'At least I'll know for sure how he feels,' she said out loud as she let herself out of her silent flat.

* * *

James let himself into his silent flat. He felt weary. Lonely. Gloomy. So dispirited, he wished he could retreat into his teenage self and crawl beneath his duvet. He shrugged off his jacket. Why was he torturing himself? He took his mobile phone from his pocket, wondering whether to ring Lucy and tell her he needed to speak to her. Urgently. Properly. Test her reaction. Stop this miserable half-life driving him crazy.

Was this really love? Cassie had made it clear from the start what she wanted from him. And that relationship had ended in tears. Lucy was so very different from his former wife. He longed to get to know her better, in every way. If only she'd let down the barriers. Stop the banter. Let him show how much he cared. If that final surrender wasn't what she wanted yet, he'd wait. As long as he knew he stood a chance.

Why had he walked away from her like that? Come back to his flat, leaving things unresolved? He'd behaved like the uptight Brit he was. That's what Cassie had accused him of being, and here he was, still too stupid to realise it.

He couldn't bear to wait until

tomorrow to see Lucy. He'd go back. Ring her and say he was outside and about to come in so she'd better hurry and fix the burglar alarm before the darned thing let the whole neighbourhood know there was an intruder at The Town Mouse.

James grabbed his duffle coat. One arm down a sleeve, he opened his front door and went out. He took the steps two at a time, pushing his other arm into the other sleeve. Jogging along the road, he checked his watch. Maybe she'd gone out. Gone for a walk. Gone to buy a Sunday paper and a bar of chocolate. Fine. But whatever happened when he got to Dexford, he wouldn't leave until they'd sorted out the situation, one way or the other.

He'd been incredibly churlish towards her. If she turned him down, his first move should be to lend an ear to her business plans.

Who am I trying to kid?

If she didn't feel the same powerful longing to be with him as he felt for her, no way would he cope with balance sheets and bank loans. Where was a flower seller when you wanted one?

* * *

The train snaked alongside the platform precisely on time. She was already standing, ready to alight. She followed the Way Out signs, pounding up the escalator to an almost-deserted concourse. She didn't have James' address. Couldn't even remember the name of the road where he lived. On the train, she'd contemplated ringing. Now, her confidence plummeted. Dustin would have contact details. Dare she ring on a Sunday, about a non-business matter?

Far better to call James and tell him she must speak to him. Urgently. And no, it couldn't wait. She selected his number. It was engaged. She stuck her mobile back in her pocket, frantically trying to recall which way the taxi went after they'd got into it that snowy Sunday night. She pulled out her phone again. If she could discover the location of the Beaufort Hotel, she could find her way to where James lived.

Lucy was walking along — doing what she cursed other people for doing: attending to her phone instead of who might be coming in the opposite direction — when she ran slap-bang into an obstruction.

'I'm so sorry.' The words rushed out in a gasp, as she instinctively shut her eyes on impact.

'No, it's entirely my fault. Sorry.' The obstruction stepped back, as if scalded.

She opened her eyes and met the full onslaught of someone else's. Heart-stoppingly gorgeous brown eyes, ringed by wickedly thick, black lashes.

'James!'

'Lucy! What in the world . . . ?'

'I was trying to ring you.'

'Me too, but your number was engaged.'

'We were trying to ring each other.' *Clever girl, Lucy. Such sharp observational skills!*

'I really need to talk to you.'

'Me too, James. Talk to you, I mean.'

'Celeste will give me hell if I make a mess of this.'

'Same here.'

'She called me something rude in Italian. I checked it on the Internet and I think she thinks I'm a numbskull.'

'Same here. I mean, she thinks I'm a numbskull, too.'

'I think I love you, Lucy. I mean, I love you, Lucy.'

'Same here. I mean, I love you, James.'

'Does that mean . . . ?' He took a step forward.

'I've brought my toothbrush.'

He pulled her close. So close, she almost couldn't breathe properly, but it didn't matter. She was in his arms. Where she belonged.

'I'm so pleased neither of us is into one-night stands,' he whispered.

'Same here. James, I think you should know I might explode if you don't kiss me.'

He tilted her face upwards. A train thundered overhead. It shuddered to a standstill as Lucy felt his lips crush hers, and Earl's Court Tube Station suddenly became the most romantic place in the world.

'Happy Christmas, darling,' she said at last.

'Thank you, lovely Lucy, but it's not Christmas yet. I haven't even bought you a gift. Not even a single red rose.'

'You're all I want for Christmas, James.'

He fumbled in his pocket and produced something small and white.

'Let's see what this says, shall we?'

She began to laugh, watching him push his fingers inside the origami fortune-telling thingy she'd made and mislaid without writing anything in it.

'How on earth did that turn up?'

'Finders, keepers. Give me a number between one and six.'

'Three.'

He pulled up a corner. 'Now a colour.'

'Pink.'

He read from beneath the flap. 'It says, *James loves you*. So it must be true.'

She held out her hand, intrigued. She looked inside each of the flaps, and read the same three words each time.

'Let's go home,' he said. 'There's so much more I want to say.'

'Me too.' Lucy lifted her face for another kiss. If this was how it felt to be a numbskull, it was so worth it.

Other titles in the
Linford Romance Library:

CHRISTMAS REVELATIONS

Jill Barry

Reluctant 1920s debutante Annabel prefers horses to suitors. When she tumbles into the path of Lawrence, Lord Lassiter, she's annoyed that this attractive man is the despised thirteenth guest joining her family for Christmas — for he has been involved in a recent scandal, and only he and his faithful valet, Norman Bassett, know the truth behind the gossip. Meanwhile, as Lawrence tries to charm Annabel, Norman has a surprise encounter with a figure from his past — one who has been keeping a secret from him for years . . .